then
you
were
gone

ALSO BY
LAUREN STRASNICK

Nothing Like You

Her and Me and You

then you were gone

LAUREN STRASNICK

SIMON PULSE

NEW YORK LONDON TORONTO SYDNEY NEW DELHI

SIMON PULSE
An imprint of Simon & Schuster Children's Publishing Division
1230 Avenue of the Americas, New York, NY 10020
First Simon Pulse paperback edition January 2014
Text copyright © 2013 by Lauren Strasnick
Cover photograph copyright © 2013 by Corbis
For information about special discounts for bulk purchases, please contact Simon & Schuster Special Sales at 1-866-506-1949 or business@simonandschuster.com.
The Simon & Schuster Speakers Bureau can bring authors to your live event.
For more information or to book an event contact the Simon & Schuster Speakers Bureau at 1-866-248-3049 or visit our website at www.simonspeakers.com.
Cover designed by Jessica Handelman
Interior designed by Hilary Zarycky
The text of this book was set in New Caledonia.
Manufactured in the United States of America
2 4 6 8 10 9 7 5 3
The Library of Congress has cataloged the hardcover edition as follows:
Strasnick, Lauren.
Then you were gone / Lauren Strasnick. — 1st Simon Pulse hardcover ed.
p. cm.
Summary: Adrienne and Dakota's long-term best friendship has been over for two years, but when Dakota goes missing, a presumed suicide, Adrienne is overwhelmed, leading to problems at school and with her boyfriend.
ISBN 978-1-4424-2715-0 (hc)
[1. Missing persons—Fiction. 2. Conduct of life—Fiction. 3. Best friends—Fiction. 4. Friendship—Fiction. 5. High schools—Fiction. 6. Schools—Fiction. 7. Family life—California—Fiction. 8. California—Fiction.] I. Title.
PZ7.S89787The 2013
[Fic]—dc23
2011040175
ISBN 978-1-4424-2716-7 (pbk)
ISBN 978-1-4424-2717-4 (eBook)

For my best girls and my ex-BFFs

then
you
were
gone

They don't love you like I love you.

—YEAH YEAH YEAHS, "MAPS"

prologue

She's standing, clutching a Coke can, dancing in front of my broken mirror. "Turn the music up?" Her moves are sluggish and slinky, and while she watches herself, she takes small, dainty sips from her soda.

"Who's singing?" I ask, leaning over, adjusting the volume on the stereo.

She puts down the Coke and swings her arms overhead. "Think I could be on the radio?"

"Sure."

She smiles. Her teeth are crooked. "Who's your favorite friend?" she asks.

"Favorite friend?"

"Yeah." Her arms drop. Her eyes are wide and she's twisting back and forth like a jittery kid. "I wanna know who you love best."

"You already know who I like best."

"Not like, love." Her mouth goes taut. "Seriously. Your favorite. Who's the person you love more than anyone else in the world?"

"Excluding my mother?"

"Obviously."

We both smile. "Hmm . . ." I stretch the moment. For once, making her wait for it. "You?"

So pleased: "Me?"

"Yes, you," I say, eyes rolling. "You're ridiculous."

She winks, turning back to her reflection.

I.

Dakota Webb.

Boys love her. Freak freshman girls worship her. She's pretty and bitchy and her dark dresses always look perfectly rumpled, as if she's slipped them on fresh from the cleaners, then rolled around in the barn for a bit.

"Adrienne?"

She wasn't always this way: shiny and cool. A baby rock god. A high school deity. She used to be just plain Dakota. Fickle, sure. A little wicked. But still, just a girl, my friend.

Right now it's seventy and sunny. I'm on my back in a plot of curly weeds. I've got my hot cell pressed to my ear and here's what I hear: my name, her voice, muffled, off-beat breathing. Squeaky noises that ride the line between giggles and sobs. I replay the message. Then again, twice more. I've heard this thing sixty times since Saturday, when I first saw her name pop up on my caller ID screen.

"Adrienne, it's me. Remember? Call back, please?"

I haven't. I've done the opposite. I've ignored her call all week.

I flip my phone shut. She's been MIA since the weekend: three successive school absences and an unsubstantiated rumor that she hasn't been home since late Sunday night. Should I be worried? Guilty?

I dial back. Four days late. I bite my tongue so hard I taste tin.

2.

"Straight to voicemail," I tell Lee.

We're in his room, on his bed. He's sliding a hand under my hip and rolling me forward. "Come closer. Come on, come'ere. Relax." He kisses me, and for a split second I feel warm, superswell, then:

"You think I should've called sooner?"

He pulls back, his lips twisted into a sloppy frown. "I don't think you should've called at all."

"Why not?"

Lee flicks me with two fingers. He grips my hips, then yanks me to the center of the bed. "You haven't talked in two years."

"Sure." But before that it was every day, all day, always— school lunches, crap snacks, R movies, heart-shaped pancakes— I loved her till she stopped loving me.

"That girl's a loon," he says.

I cup Lee's cheek. I like Lee's cheek.

"And her band sucks."

They don't. I wish they did. They make pretty, moody music. Music that makes me want to screw everyone, then stab myself in the heart. "You're just jealous."

"No, *you* are." He undoes my top two blouse buttons. "And you shouldn't be."

He's right. I want to look hot and talk hot and do bad things and be forgiven. I want to sing and swing my hips and make the whole world love me.

"Hey."

"Hmm?"

Another kiss. And this one's slow and so warm and Lee's clutching my top with two fists. "Hate this thing . . ." Baby buttercups on dingy white silk. Peter Pan collar. Pearl buttons. "Shit taste in shirts," he coos, slipping both hands under my bra. Then, "Love these things."

I laugh, looking sideways, to the mirror above Lee's bureau. There I am: splotchy from all the groping. Lee's in his soccer uniform, his head buried between my breasts. A trophy, catching late light through Lee's bedroom window, reflects spots onto both our faces.

"Hey, Lee?"

"Hey, what?"

"Make me a sandwich?"

"Sexy words."

"I skipped lunch."

He groans. Moves down my body. Pushes up off the bed. "Extra mustard? You want Havarti or Swiss?"

I screw my face into an appreciative grin. "You're a good boyfriend."

He scrunches one eye shut. Adjusts his shorts. "Havarti, right?"

"No. Swiss," I say softly. "Please, thank you, you're the best."

3.

"Drink this," Kate instructs.

We're at school, on the quad, sipping gin from a Sprite bottle. Kate's eating leftover pad see ew out of a Tupperware container. "Bite?"

I nod, leaning forward. Kate shovels a glossy heap of noodle into my mouth. I chew, and watch her watch the smoggy skyline. Sun, clouds, brown mountains—all hidden behind a gray, hazy film.

"Imports."

"Hmm?"

She points. "Palm trees." Picks a baby carrot off my untouched plate. "They don't belong and now they're dying."

I follow her gaze. "They don't look sick."

"Fungal disease," she says, gnawing the carrot. "Here, finish this." She passes the noodles. I take the tub. Another bite. "Good, right?" Her eyes fix on my mouth.

"New Thai place on La Brea." She dumps the last of the Sprite/gin down her throat, then says: "I feel sorry for them."

"Who?"

"*Hello.*" She knocks my head with her knuckles. "The trees." We stare at each other for a bit. Kate has drunk eyes. Her blond waves look windswept and shiny. "Am I boring you?"

"I—"

"I'm boring you."

"No." I'm itchy and restless and worried. "You haven't . . . ?" I pull my cardigan close to my body. "I mean . . . you haven't heard anything, have you?"

"About?"

I shrug. Kate's loyal and loves me and hates: "Dakota Webb."

"Oh, Knox." She groans, leaning back. "Stop, okay? Stop obsessing. She's *fine*. She's in a band. Rock people pull this shit. She'll turn up, I swear it."

But that voicemail. That sad, screwy message.

"Knox?"

"Hmm?"

We look left.

Wyatt Shaw, Kate's crush, in the distance. He's skinny, Wyatt. Tall, too, and everlastingly clad in military boots, a navy peacoat, and thick-rimmed glasses. Dandy meets suburban punk. "I love you, I love you, I love you," Kate whispers. Then she extends a leg, tripping him.

"What the fuck?" He stumbles, rights himself, then ogles Kate quizzically.

She winks. No shit.

"What the hell was that?" I ask, half freaked, half impressed.

"I can't get him to like me," she says—zero irony. We both watch Wyatt stagger off, dazed, amazed.

"Yeah, well, you're on the right track," I say, patting her thigh enthusiastically. "Next time, sucker punch him in the kidney. Guys love that."

She laughs. Looks at me.

"Right?"

Her smile withers. She pokes my shoulder. "Hey. Promise me something."

"Hmm?"

"If she calls again. You won't pick up."

"Katie, *no*." I lean forward. "No. Why would you ask that?"

"Because. She's trouble. She's messy and gets herself into stupid situations and then people like *you* have to clean up her shit." She grimaces. "Remember when we met? You and me?"

"That was different," I say. "That was *me*, the mess." Freshly dumped by D. Webb. "I was lonely."

"You were so sad."

"I'm okay now. I have you. And Lee."

I expect a smile or some sort of off-kilter joke, but Kate just looks at me, really *looks* at me, and says this: "She's not better than you. You know that, right?"

I wince. "I don't think that."

"Yes," she says, rocking my shoulder with one hand. "You do."

On the walk to lit, I'm on my cell, dialing and redialing Dakota. *Voicemail, voicemail, voicemail.* Her cracked outgoing message? "Whom the Gods love die young." New recording? Old? I shove my phone in my pocket and slip into class. The bell shrieks like a banshee.

Lit with Nick Murphy. Everyone worships the guy because he's young, cute, and yes, believe it: He makes learning fun. He's married to an equally likable, preggo math teacher named Gwen. Blond and cheery. Kate has her for trig.

"Jane Eyre, people. Take out your books."

I'm a shit student, solid Cs, but I'll read pretty much anything: comics, trashy romance, *The Iliad*. Murphy's class is the one class I like. I like books. I like the guy telling me which books to read. But now, with Dakota gone and my brain mashed and scrambled, I can barely read the backs of beauty products. My focus is shit. Murphy talks but I don't listen. I riffle through my bag for *Jane*.

"Anyone?" Murphy rubs his head, back to front, smiling

while he does it. "Anyone with mind-blowingly awesome perspective on Brontë?" *There*, again, back to front. He does it daily. He punctuates sentences with that move. Such a nothing gesture—*rub-a-dub-dub*—but he looks so freakin' affable (F-able?) doing it. "Who likes Jane?" A bunch of hands fly up. "Yeah? What do you like about her?"

Meg Rofé—tiny nose, sweet voice—screams, "Orphan!"

Everyone laughs. Murphy nods. "Sure, orphans. *Likable*. What else?"

"No boning what's-his-name." Lynn Rofé, Meg's twin. "The guy with the wife."

"'Boning,'" Murphy muses. "Choice word."

Julian Boyd, Dakota's quasi boyfriend/bandmate, sits two rows down and one aisle over. If I lean backward and a little left, my view is perfect. He looks miserable. He always looks miserable—under-eye circles, down-turned mouth—but today, he looks puffy and red and sincerely forlorn. Is *she* the one fucking his face up? Is he obsessed, perplexed, down, and done wrong by? Maybe he just really hates *Jane Eyre*.

Lee skips Intro to Economics and meets me behind the gym in the cozy little patch of cacti and rocks that overlooks the school pool. We meet here during free/not-free periods because it's sunny and secluded, and because Lee likes the smell of chlorine.

"Hi," he says, clutching my hands and hips, kissing my lips, ears, neck. "You wanna stay here or go to my car?"

"Here, please," I say, sounding horse but feeling high. "The sun feels nice."

"It does," he agrees, backing me into the stucco siding. "How much time do we have?"

I shove my chin past his shoulder and check my watch. "Forty minutes." Our stomachs are flush. "Pull up your shirt?" I ask. "Just a little?"

Skin-to-skin contact. What Lee and I do best: talk nonsense and push up against each other. "How's that?"

"Good."

Eighteen months. That's how long we've been doing this. I met Kate in ceramics toward the end of sophomore year. She and Lee were close. "He's a great guy," she said. "He wants to F you," she joked. He had floppy hair and rich parents. His dad wrote action scripts. His mom, an ex-actress, had done a bunch of crappy comedies in the eighties. But Lee seemed well-adjusted. He liked puppies and sports. He didn't drink very much or smoke, or do drugs or spend excessively. He made me feel wanted and safe.

"Am I driving you to Kate's later?" He wraps one arm around my waist.

I say, "Come get me at six?" And, "Can we stop for pie on the way?"

"Pie?" Lee laughs.

"We're dessert this week."

"Pie, then." He snaps my bra strap.

Home.

Blue stucco, rusty gate, potted succulents, lantana shrubs.

"Hello?" I slam the back door, drop my bag by the hutch, and kick off my flats. "Who's here?"

"Me." Sam. Mom's boyfriend. "Kitchen."

I follow the smell of sizzling shallots and find Sam hovering over a skillet with a wooden spatula.

"Hi, kid."

"Hey. Mom home?"

"On her way."

Sam is always home. He does web design out of the walk-in closet by the half bath down the hall. Mom converted the space into an office for him late last year (sloping ceilings with two tiny windows that look out onto our neighbor's pretty mosaic garden—broken glass, bird baths, Technicolor tile). Before that, it was my favorite place to read and take naps.

"Want some?" He passes me a plate with some roughly cut apple.

I take a slice. "It's good," I say. Supercrunchy and tart.

"Farmer's market. In that lot by the bank off Glendale."

Sam and Mom have been happily unwed for ten years now. My real dad lives in upstate New York. Which is, whatever, fine.

"You okay?" He's eyeing me sideways.

I grab a glass off the drying rack and fill it with tap water. "Dakota's missing."

He adjusts the burner heat. Doesn't flinch. "What do you mean, missing?"

"I mean, she's missing. Like, full-on gone. Like, troll freshman girls are spreading hideous, shitty rumors about—" I stop myself.

"Have you tried Emmett?" Emmett: Dakota's stepdad. Less dad, more landlord.

"No."

"Want me to call him?"

"*No.*"

Sam spends three seconds looking somber. He's facing me. He looks so slender and serious. He's wearing the apron I tie-dyed for Mom for her forty-third birthday. "I saw her," he says.

I'm mid-guzzle. I swallow, slam my cup down, and wipe my mouth dry. "What do you mean, you saw her? When?"

"Sunday night. Outside the Echo."

My insides seize. "You *saw* her?"

"I was picking up pizza for me and Mom, and she was getting dropped off."

"You didn't tell me that." I roll it over in my brain for a bit. "Wait, why didn't you tell me that?"

He shrugs, turning back to the stove. "Seemed pretty

15

minor. And I didn't—" One quick stir. "I thought it might upset you."

I shake my head, embarrassed. Suddenly so see-through. "Why would you think that?"

He looks up, suppressing a grin.

"Why are you smiling?" I say, sounding snappish. "This isn't funny."

"Adrienne, honey." He pauses, tossing some salt into the sauce. "That girl doesn't exactly trigger your inner angel."

I flinch.

Sam softens. "No, look, she was pissed and kicking the crap out of some lunatic's car."

"Lunatic?"

"No, I don't know. Just some guy. Or girl, maybe?"

I laugh. Involuntarily. Sam does too.

"Typical."

"Right?" He ruffles my hair. "Honey, I'm sure she's all right. She does this. Goes away. Comes back." He looks at me. "You gonna be okay?"

I nod, shaking off my shit mood and stepping back. "So what's with the white mess in the pan?"

"White *mess*?" He picks up his spatula. "No, no . . . white *perfection*." He smiles and bites a bit of sauce off the spatula tip. "You're eating out?"

"Supper Club," I say. Weekly potluck at Kate's place. "Can I have some money? I have to pick up a pie on the way."

He pulls a wad of cash from his pocket and hands me a twenty.

"Thanks," I say. Smile. On second thought: "Hey."

"Hmm?"

"She was *kicking* the car?"

"Yup, the wheel."

"You're sure you didn't see the guy?"

"Sorry."

Discouraged, I start down the hall to my room. Then, "Hey, Sam?"

"Yeah?"

"You remember what kind of car?"

I hear a couple of pots clink together, then the faucet goes on. "It was a Bug."

"A bug?"

"Yeah. An old VW Beetle. I had the same car when I was sixteen."

Huh. "Color?"

"Yellow," Sam shouts. Then, so soft I almost don't hear: "Mine was red."

4.

In my room, on my bureau, a photograph. I've got dozens of these, but keep coming back to this one: Dakota and me, fourteen, side by side on my stoop. She's blowing a kiss at the camera. Her lips are purple and puckered, her eyes lined with liquid black. She's wearing boots and blue tights and a dark, floral mini. I'm in an oversized white tank and taupe shorts and she's shoving me down. My head's to my knees and she's gleeful, her eyes shining.

5.

Kate lives in Hancock Park, where they've got streetlamps and wide lawns and big stone homes. Her house is tall and covered with soft green moss. She has two parents, a pool, and a potbellied pig named Darla. Every Thursday we make a shit-ton of food, serve it up on nice china, and drink ourselves sick.

Tonight it's me, Lee, Kate, Teddy Walker, Margaret Yates, and pretty, wispy Alice Reed, who's across the table, next to Lee, fake smoking a giant breadstick.

"She has it all," Kate whispers, smelling like crackers and strawberry gloss and Nag Champa incense. "Brains, boobs . . ." Kate's being shitty. Alice Reed is flat and dumb. "Feels nice, right? Rounding out our social circle?"

"Round enough as is, no?"

"We're too exclusionary," Kate says, sighing. I smear a dab of pie custard onto her nose. "Mmm," she says, stretching her tongue over her upper lip. "Chocolate."

A piercing laugh from across the table.

"Do it again," shrieks Lee. Alice sucks, inhales, then exhales—forming her mouth into a pleasing, pouty O.

"Bravo."

Smoke ring pantomime. We all clap.

Teddy Walker—rich, stuck-up, into boys, into clothes—passes Alice the lentil salad. "Here," he says. "Smoke this."

She takes the dish, serves herself, serves my boyfriend.

"A toast!" Kate's filling my cup to its brim with red wine.

"To?" I say, slurping the overflow off the top.

She faces me and, with a hand to her heart, says: "You."

"Oh, to *me*?" I fan my face with my free hand. "Really?"

"To Adrienne!" everyone screams, gulping wine and clanking cups.

Kate's fat, surly piggy waddles past me and plops down on the Persian carpet.

"To Darla!" shouts Lee.

"To Darla!" we echo. And for the first time all week I feel the teensiest bit happy.

We keep toasting. To sunny skies and starry nights. To taco trucks and cigarette breadsticks. To Dr. Strange, our principal. To Gwen Murphy's baby. To the Cannons, Kate's parents, for supplying us with booze but then taking our car keys. To Margaret's debate win. To Wyatt Shaw, Kate's crush. "To Dakota Webb!" screams Teddy. And with that, my buzz fizzles.

"Where is that girl?" Alice asks.

"On the lam," says Teddy.

"Yeah? What's she running from?"

"Sex," he says, laughing.

"Running from sex?" I say, super annoyed while everyone giggles. "Not funny." I rearrange my silverware. "Doesn't even make any sense . . ."

"No, wait—" Teddy again. "Drugs."

More laughter.

"Running *from* drugs?" he ponders. "Running *with* drugs?"

"Moving on," Kate interjects. "Pass the peas, please?"

No peas. But Lee passes the lentils and the bread basket.

I watch my lap. Sip some wine. Kate drills two knuckles into my kneecap. "Yeah?"

"You're wanted."

I look up. More giggles. More plate-passing and blue-cheese/tomato-salad/dry-salami/lentil-eating. Lee's wiggling one brow at me, mock seductively. I grin a little. *What?* I mouth. He points left.

"Bathroom," I say to Kate.

"Sure, slut."

I stand. Lee follows. We go to the guest bath down the hall. Lee locks the door. Lifts me onto the vanity. "You okay?" he asks.

"I'm okay," I say.

21

"You wanna talk about it?"

"Nope." I lean forward, rub my nose against his nose. "Eskimos," I whisper.

"Eskimos," he says back. He licks my face. I kick him closer with one foot. We kiss slow, so slow, the slowest, most slippery kiss. I wrap my arms around his neck; my body settles. "Let's stay here for a while, okay?"

"Okay," Lee says.

I shut my eyes.

6.

Everyone's saying it: *suicide*. All those sneaky *s* sounds.

From the *LA Times* blog:

> Eighteen-year-old Langley senior and Los Angeles resident Dakota Webb has gone missing. Webb fronts the local indie band Dark Star. Just last month, Dark Star played to packed audiences during its Monday-night residency at the downtown all-ages venue the Smell.

> Webb's abandoned Jeep was discovered early Friday morning in a pay lot off Pacific Coast Highway. A note, allegedly written by Webb, was found inside the vehicle. The note's contents have not been disclosed.

Last month, another Los Angeles teen, Crossroads sophomore Cassidy Chang, disappeared. Her Ford sedan was found in the same beach parking lot.

"I'm taking you home," Lee tells me. He's holding one hand and Kate's holding the other. "You're gonna be okay," they say. And: "Adrienne, hey, don't go crazy with this."

Principal Strange, moments ago: "Let's say a silent prayer for our shining star, Dakota Webb."

Two squad cars are parked by the auditorium exit.

"Knox, hey, they have a note, that's all."

Absolutely not, no way, not possible. "She would never—not *ever*—" I hear myself stutter. Only, I dunno, would she? "Pills before razors. Razors before ropes," we used to joke. But drowning? Rocks in pockets? She didn't even like the beach. "You guys?" I'm being escorted somewhere. Lee's car? We're crossing the quad. Kate's palm trees swoosh overhead.

"Knox." Which one says this? Both their faces look flat and gloomy. "Knox, it's okay . . . sit."

I get in. Lee's to my left. Kate stays outside, one hand touching the car door.

"It's hot in here, are you hot?" I roll down my window. I'm shaky and flying and spaced out. Two girls dressed in funeral black shiver and clutch each other by the old oak near the exit. "You're coming, right?"

"I gotta stay," Kate says, leaning forward, kissing my cheek. "Call you later?"

I feel like a fucking hot-air balloon. "She didn't kill herself," I blurt. Lee rubs my shoulder. "No way would she copy some sad sophomore from Crossroads."

At home, Lee sits with me in the den.

"You want anything?"

We're waiting on my mother, who's heading home from a design job in the Valley.

"Is this my fault?" I ask Lee.

"No." The *o* in the 'no' is long and insistent.

"I waited. I waited *four days* to call back. She wanted help and I just—"

"You don't know what she wanted," Lee says. And, "Hey." His hand moves to my thigh. "She wasn't nice, Knox. She was shitty to you."

True and not true. She was shitty, sure. Also? She was funny and magnetic and nutso-crazy fun. "Don't say 'was.'" I flick his fingers away.

Keys jingle, the door creaks, and: "Hello? Babe?"

Lee stands, says, "In here," then greets my frazzled mom with a quick, loose hug.

"You guys okay?" She's at my side now, rocking me, smothering my face with kisses. "Babe, you okay?"

I say, "Yes, okay," then shoot Lee a frosty look. Mom's face is inches from my face. "Oh, babe." She looks so broken-hearted. Everything about her looks gray and miserable, even her hair. "She wasn't a happy girl."

I stand up, stepping backward. "Stop saying 'was.'" I'm furious and dizzy and completely perplexed. Why's no one asking questions? What if she's been abducted or hurt or worse? What about the yellow Bug Sam saw Sunday night? "Where's Sam?" I say.

"On his way."

"You called him? You told him?"

"Babe, come'ere, yes." She clutches my head to her chest. Something wet drips into my hair part.

"Are you *crying?*" I sit up. "Stop it." She's blubbering. Her boobs are heaving and she's swiping her tears away faster than they're falling. "We don't know anything yet. Don't act like that."

"She was so small, when you guys were kids, remember? Just—really tiny."

"Stop!" I have to sit on my hands to keep myself from slapping her. The sadder she gets, the more miserable I feel. I don't want to picture small, sweet Dakota. Ten years old—stringy hair, at the back of the bus with her lunch pail. That girl faded once puberty hit, and in her place grew something dark and shiny and diamond-hard.

"She needed *parents*, better guidance, love—"

"Please," I plead, and Lee yanks me to my feet, pulling

me away from my mother and into the kitchen.

"Look at me," he says sharply, grabbing my chin and backing me against the fridge. "She loved her too, okay?"

Immediate remorse. Lee exhales and I wind my arms around his torso.

"We don't know anything yet, okay?"

"Okay," I say. I cling a little tighter.

7.

Sam spends all Saturday afternoon buying me crap. Stuff I normally love that I just can't choke down now—chocolate croissants from Casbah Café, hazelnut gelato from that place on Hyperion, a fish taco from my favorite stand on Sunset. I take two bites and he finishes the rest. Later on, we walk the Silver Lake Reservoir twice. It takes about an hour, and I make Sam tell me all over again each detail from the previous Sunday.

"She kicked the car, you're sure?"

"Right, a couple of hard kicks," Sam says.

"And you're sure it was yellow?"

"Absolutely," he says with a firm nod. "Yellow and dented and old."

I watch the lake: stagnant, glossy, black. Nothing like seawater. Still, I make myself see it: Dakota floating faceup. Facedown. Drifting along the cement shoreline. The image won't stick. Doesn't feel real.

. . .

Sunday's like this:

Lee picks me up at ten a.m. and takes me to Kate's place. They've plotted my perfect day: packaged snacks from Little Tokyo (rice crackers, red-bean cakes, mochi balls), Zeppelin and Deep Purple on the stereo (seventies metal, my fave), G&Ts by the pool (a tradition Kate cooked up last year after reading *Play It As It Lays* by Didion: afternoon cocktails, sixties casual-wear, bleak tête-à-tête). Kate even gives me my very own copy of *The Secret Language of Eating Disorders* by Peggy Claude-Pierre, a book she's been inexplicably obsessed with since tenth grade health ed.

"Thanks," I say. I flip through the book, sip my G&T, watch Kate and Lee stuff their faces with powdery rolls of mochi.

"Have some."

"No."

They look at each other. They look at the pool, they look at the pig. "Darla," Kate coos, and Darla waddles across the lawn, toward me. "She's incredibly sensitive," Kate insists, licking white dust off her fingertips. "She wants to kiss away your woes . . ."

I pat the pig's rump, then scooch forward, slipping my feet into the cool pool.

"Should we swim?" Lee says.

"That's okay."

"Play something?" Kate offers. "Boggle? Apples to Apples?"

"No."

"Want to go somewhere?"

"Not really."

"Bake something?"

"Uh-uh."

They're stumped. Wound up. They want me fine again but can't figure out a way to make me feel fine.

"What do you miss?" Lee asks, abruptly.

"What do you mean?" I say back.

"About Dakota." He's forcing a small mound of dirt between two clay patio tiles. "What, specifically, do you miss?"

"I don't know," I mumble, unable to come up with anything definitive on the spot. She wasn't the nicest person, or the most loyal or loving or true, but we spent years knowing only each other. Why can't that count?

"Can I use your computer?" I say to Kate.

"It's in the den," she says, reaching for my hand and squeezing my pinkie. "Knox, hey."

"Hmm?"

"It's gonna be okay," she says.

I give a small smile and squeeze back. Then I pull my feet from the pool.

• • •

Later, around nine, Lee parks his mom's Range Rover half a mile from my house. "You're sure you feel like it?" he asks, killing the engine. We're on the edge of Elysian, overlooking Dodger Stadium.

"Sure I'm sure." I climb over the armrest and into the backseat. "Get my jeans?" I undo my fly and let Lee tug down my pants. I pull off my cardigan and frayed white tank. "Take off your shirt," I tell him. He doesn't. Instead, he kisses me.

Is this love? Shouldn't I feel happy or high or both? Is Lee's love worthy of song lyrics and sonnets? Is this what love was like for Jane and Rochester? Or Dakota and Julian? Did their love feel safe and smothering, like a blanket?

"Adrienne?"

"Hmm?"

He slides a hand between my legs.

8.

Monday, and I'm back at school pondering cars. Everyone here looks pale and shell-shocked. The place even smells off—different disinfectant? Whatever it is, it smells sad.

"You're here." It's Kate, at my locker.

"Yeah, well, it was either this, or stay home and stare at the ceiling."

She sips her cafeteria coffee. "There's an assembly last period. Suicide prevention."

My stomach goes bananas. "Walk me to lit?"

We stroll. The halls are silent, like church. We stop just shy of Murphy's classroom. "You've got a sub," Kate says, peering past me.

I whip around. "That guy." Bald, spacey suspender dude. "That guy subbed my human development class last spring. Super-hands-on."

"Really?" Kate passes me her coffee cup, then uses both hands to tuck her T-shirt into her jeans.

"I'm kidding."

"Oh." She takes the cup back. "Maybe Gwen had her kid?"

"Maybe," I say, picturing a squished newborn version of Nick Murphy. "When do you have trig?"

"After lunch. So we'll see, I guess."

Babies. Suicides. "Life cycles, right?"

Kate blinks, tilts her head, walks off. I take two steps toward class, then, rethinking, quickly pivot and head outside to the student lot.

Within minutes, I'm weaving between cars, searching for rusty and round and yellow. I touch the ones I like. A diesel Mercedes. A Carmengia. An old Land Rover. A khaki Jeep. I walk and I weave and I wade for a while, but no yellow Bug materializes.

Suicide-prevention brochures, warning-sign checklists, crisis-center locations, *We miss you, Dakota Webb.*

I'm at the back of the auditorium with Kate, Lee, and Alice Reed. Lee's holding my hand but I don't like how it feels: clammy and warm and too tight. Dr. Strange is at the podium babbling mopey nonsense. Two kids two rows back are heatedly debating Dakota's vanishing: suicide vs. murder vs. runaway madness. I get up.

"Where're you going?" Kate whispers.

"Bathroom."

"I'll come." She starts to stand—

"Don't. Please?"

—then drops back down.

"I'll be back. I'm okay. I just—I can pee on my own."

I'm off. Out the tall double doors, into the blue, bright hallway, past the restrooms, out the exit. I'm not even sure where I'm headed, but at least now no one's watching me or clutching my hot hand.

I end up across the quad, Dakotaland, where the weirdos hang out. And look, there's Julian Boyd, crouched on the ground, five feet from a Hacky Sack circle, smoking and biting his cuticles and just looking generally low.

I bum a cigarette. I don't smoke, but I bum one off some lanky skateboarder wearing a belt made of rope. He lights it for me. I inhale. My head fills with white space. "Hi, hello," I hear myself saying, not to the skateboarder, but to Julian. He doesn't respond. So I try again. "Julian," I say, louder this time. He looks at me, grinds his cigarette into the grass, and walks off.

I wonder what kind of car he drives.

9.

Mom is at the kitchen counter, chopping white onion for guacamole. ". . . the props guy is new. We met up with Locations earlier—we're trying to get a concrete feel for the space." She stops, nibbles a piece of parsley, turns to me. "Too much?"

"What?" I look up from my mound of mashed avocado.

"Work talk. You look bored."

"I'm just"—I laugh a little—"out of my freakin' mind, ya know?"

She cracks one knuckle. Passes some parsley. "Eat that. It'll ground you."

I eat it. "Tastes like weeds," I say, swallowing, grabbing two tomatoes out of the sink. "What am I doing with these?"

"Cut 'em in half, scoop the seeds out."

"Can I have that?" I wiggle my finger at the serrated knife.

She passes it. Wipes her teary onion eyes. "I called Emmett earlier."

I stop slicing. Look up. "Why?"

"To check in. See if he needs anything." I make a sour face. *"What?"* she says. "He has no one."

"Whose fault is that?"

"Babe."

"Just sayin'. No one's nominating the guy for any Stepdad of the Year awards."

"Shush, please." More parsley. "Dakota wasn't the easiest kid."

"Wasn't?"

"Isn't."

"So," I say, nudging tomato sludge into the trash with my nails. "How'd he sound?"

"Weird. Which is right, right? How else would he sound?"

"Weird, like, how?"

"Weird, like, *fine*, I guess. Just thought he'd sound a bit more shaken up."

"Well, what'd you talk about?" I ask.

"I just, ya know, offered my sympathies. Asked if we could bring anything by."

"And?"

"He said 'no thanks.' That he appreciated the offer. You done?" She gestures at my avocado/tomato mash.

"Here." I pass both. She dumps everything into one bowl.

Does some quick mixing. Squeezes two lemons. "Did he sound sorry?" I say.

"What do you mean?"

"Like, did he sound *sorry*? That she's gone?"

"You can't tell that sort of thing over the phone." She digs a chip into the guac and waves it at me. "Here. Taste test." Then, "Besides, people process their crap differently."

"It's good," I manage, mouth full. And, "I thought everyone processed their crap exactly the same."

"Funny," she says, pulling me close, pushing my face against her chest.

"Can't breathe," I cry, writhing, whining.

"Shut up, please?" She kisses my forehead, hugs me harder. "I need to squeeze my kid."

10.

My back is flat against Lee's locker. He's nuzzling me.

"I called twice last night."

I heard. Saw my cell screen blink. But the thought of talking—to Lee, to Kate—just seemed unnecessarily exhausting. "I was busy."

"With what?"

I shrug. Lee pulls back. He has that glazed look guys get when they're super-sexed-up. "Can I see you tonight?"

He's high off Range Rover Sunday. "Don't know," I say. "Maybe?" I stupidly thought sex with Lee might obliterate that relentless tug in my gut, but—

"*Maybe?*"

Didn't work.

"Do you know anyone who drives a yellow Bug?" I say, switching subjects.

"A Bug?"

"Yeah."

"What, like, a Volkswagen?"

"Uh-huh."

"No." He thinks about it. "I mean, maybe. Not sure. Why?"

"Sam saw Dakota last Sunday in a Bug. Or, getting out of a Bug. She was fighting with someone."

"Sam *saw* her?"

I nod, speedy now. High, almost. "He talked to an officer this weekend. They're looking into it."

"Huh."

"They want to talk to me, too."

"The police? But you don't know anything."

"Her phone records. They saw the call." He doesn't say anything back, so I talk on. "The Bug, though. That's, like, a lead, right?"

"I guess."

"You guess?" I step backward and let go a small, irritated huff. "You don't think that's a little strange? Dakota gets into some huge blowout with some mystery guy, then, *poof*, she just disappears?"

"I dunno, Knox. Sure, maybe." He pauses, readjusts his backpack. "You know she brought mescaline to Teddy's barbecue last year? His parents were there. Who brings psychedelics to a family barbecue?"

"She was at Teddy's? Do they even know each other?"

"Knox." His cross-eyes say I'm missing his point. "She screwed Anna Clark's boyfriend. That guy who tours with Jason Sheer?"

"The guitar player? Isn't that guy old?"

"Bass. And he's twenty-four. She went home with him after a Dark Star show."

"How do you know that? You don't even know those people."

"Chris Clark, Anna's brother. He's on my soccer team." A beat. Lee makes a strained face. "I just . . ."

"What?" I say. "You *what*?"

"I don't know." He walks, mussing his hair with one hand. "I kinda think . . ." Laughs. "I kinda think it's a big pile of horseshit. I think she's fine, I think she's fucking with everyone, I think you're falling for it. I'm watching you—you're getting all obsessive and invested and—"

"I'm not obsessive. Jesus, Lee. I'm flipping the fuck out because my friend might be—"

"Your *friend*?"

One of my cheeks—the left one?—is throbbing as if it's been hit. "Fuck you." My eyes pool. I turn on one heel and walk toward the restroom.

"Adrienne."

I don't stop.

"Hey, *Adrienne*." Lee catches up with me, tugs on my

arm, flips me around. "Stop, okay?" Wipes my wet cheeks. "Stop crying, I'm sorry." He kisses me. Our mouths are hot and soggy. "I just—" He pulls back, head shaking, chin wrinkling. "I don't like her."

I want to scratch, smack, set something on fire.

"I wish—I want you to forget her."

"*Forget* her?" More irate tears. He curls an arm around me. I try wriggling free.

"Stop squirming."

"You don't get it."

"I do, I get it, you're worried." His face goes lax. "Adrienne, I just—I want you to feel better."

"Well, I can't."

We just stand there, kids staring, school bells blaring. I keep crying. Lee takes my hand and I'm too tired to stop him. "Can I see you later?"

"No."

"Why not?"

My chest heaves. "Dinner with my mother." Lies.

He pulls me forward. "Tell me you love me."

"No."

"Knox . . ."

"Tell me you're sorry," I say.

"I am. Already said it."

"Say it again."

"Look at me."

I look at him. Baby skin, sparse stubble, a tiny pimple on his upper lip. "I love you," he whispers. And it's true, he means it. "I'm sorry," he says. "You believe me?"

I relax slightly. "I guess."

"You're sure?"

"Yes," I say, pressing my nose against his cold cotton jersey. "I'm sure."

II.

Brit lit. Suspender Sub still here. We're doing absolutely nothing in class—reading chapters aloud out of *Jane Eyre*—so I watch Julian watch the floor while wondering what he knows. Who he is. Does he look guilty? Grief-stricken? He's so stupidly pretty. Dirty red hair that droops at the sides and sticks up on top. Freckles like Kate. Dakota used to back him into lockers and suck his lower lip in front of everyone. Now he's here with his Brontë book and all I see is sex.

Bell.

He bolts. I grab my bag and tailgate him. Kate's waiting outside and blocks me as Julian slips past.

"Murphy had the baby. It's a girl."

"Oh." He's gone now, out of sight.

"They named her Adeline."

"Huh."

She slaps my upper arm.

"*Ow*. What the hell, why'd you do that?"

"You okay?"

"I *was* fine, *fuck*. Now I hurt."

"Sorry, I just—" Her cheeks go pink. "You weren't looking at me."

My eyes flick to her face.

"You going tonight?"

"Where?" I ask, rubbing the throb out of my arm.

"Candlelight vigil."

"For?"

Her brow bounces up. Duh, D. Webb.

"Oh," I say, smarting. "Seems a little premature."

"Right? Bury the girl first." Kate laughs a little too quickly, then stares for a bit before changing the subject. "Come on, you're free this period. Help me stalk Wyatt Earp."

I glance out the window. There's a fat camera guy hovering in front of a navy van with a satellite. A suited woman waves a mic in the faces of two tiny freshman.

Kate smooshes her nose against the glass. "Fuck, Channel Five?" Then, softly: "Dakota gets a camera crew. Of course."

12.

I toss my keys on the bureau, switch on my yellow bedside lamp, and hit play on a mix I made earlier this week: Keren Ann, Olivia Ruiz, Yael Naim, Carla Bruni. Girlie French music. Folk and pop. I can't understand a word of it, but it makes me feel dreamy and sentimental and tints everything really rosy.

For a while, I don't do anything but listen. I get down on the floor on my back and just lie there. I watch the ceiling. I flip to my side and watch the wall. Then, feeling restless, I get up. Drink half a glass of water. Change into sleep stuff. Creep downstairs to Sam's office and switch on his computer.

Ping.

Sam has video footage of Dakota, I'm sure of it. The first five years of his relationship with my mother are taped, digitized, and double-saved to his hard drive. I click the folder titled *Home Movies* and run a search for "Dakota." Nothing. I try "Adrienne." A zillion files flash in my face: "Adrienne Seven," "Adrienne Swing Set," "Adrienne & Rach" (Mom). I try searching "Adrienne Nine", then "Adrienne Ten" (prime DW years)—more nothing. I type "Adrienne Twelve," and there, finally, a file. I open it.

Me, Mom—getting ready for Ally Rothbaum's bat mitzvah.

Wrong. Moving on.

"Adrienne Eleven."

Dakota.

We're kids. She's braiding my hair. We're in a tent with three billion throw pillows, a bottle of bubbly water, and a cordless phone.

"Face me, come on, guys, say something cute."

"Something cute!" Dakota screams, smiling huge, then frowning dramatically. I laugh and I laugh, so Sam laughs too. The picture cuts out.

Two more clips: "D&A" and "Adrienne B-Day Fifteen." In the first, I'm fourteen, maybe? My hair chin-length and tinged red. I'm leaning against the kitchen counter eating a fat slice of pepperoni.

"Dakota honey?" Mom says this. She's fixing one of her weird-looking sprouted salads. D wanders into frame. She looks young. No boobs. Her face still soft.

"Yeah?"

Mom picks an eyelash off her cheek then hands her the salad bowl. "Stick this on the table, will you?"

"Rach, wave," Sam says. Mom waves.

"Do I have to have salad?" I ask.

"Yep."

"I *love* salad," Dakota sings, picking a sprout out of the bowl and nibbling at it seductively.

"Babe, put the camera down?" Mom's got a fistful of silverware and she's bumping the drawer shut with one hip. "Get the lasagna out of the oven? Come on, we're eating."

"Okay, all right," Sam says. The picture drops.

Last one: "Adrienne B-Day Fifteen." I remember this. Not long before our breakup. A few weeks, maybe? We're at Dar Maghreb on Sunset. Moroccan. Chicken pie with powdered sugar, tiled walls, belly dancers. Mom and Dakota on either side of me. Everyone looking pretty and made-up: three sets of red lips. Smooth hair.

Dakota—boobs now, layered bob—says, "We do this with our hands?" She means *eat*—no utensils.

Mom: "Indeed, we do."

I reach for something. Chicken pie? Flatbread? Dakota stops me. "Birthday girl! Let me do that!"

"Let you do *what*?"

"I'm gonna feed you," she says brightly. She reaches down,

pinches some pie between her fingertips, and raises it to my mouth. "Open up."

"No." I laugh.

"Why, come on, don't be scared," she coos. "Come on. Open your mouth."

"Be nice," says Sam.

Dakota looks directly at the lens, says, "I *am* nice." Then she pries my lips apart while I squirm. "There you go, baby." She smooshes the chicken onto my cheek, missing my mouth completely.

Freeze frame.

13.

"Can I have one of those?"

Freak section. I'm bumming a cigarette off a girl wearing an apron as a dress.

"Here." She passes me her pack and a stubby pink lighter.

I help myself, light up, say, "Thanks." Today I dressed the part: dark brown sweater over black tights. And I lined my eyes with kohl.

Hours later I'm in the computer lab googling like a maniac. I find an online Dakota tribute: an ultra simple website with Dakota photos and some super sappy reader comments. I can barely look at any of it. Except the video. There's a shitty, shaky video of Dakota performing somewhere. I dig through my bag, find my headphones, and plug into the computer. She's singing softly. She sounds like a gurgling baby. Below her are a gazillion bobbing heads. People love her. *I* love her.

She's pretty and perfect and up onstage she makes magic. *Made* magic?

New website. New video. This one's overexposed. Dakota with Dark Star in some stark rehearsal space. Daytime. She's barefaced. Her blond hair limp and long and just so fucking glorious. She's harmonizing with her own recorded vocals. Swaying slightly. Looking girlish and sexy while she smiles at Julian, who's got his jean-jacketed back to the camera.

"How's that?" she asks, stopping, leaping up.

"Awful," says some guy off camera. Everyone laughs. Dakota's face widens. She's happy, laughing, flinging herself onto Julian's lap. The camera rotates. His hands are on her face. They're kissing and grinning. Someone throws a guitar pick across the room. My heart bleeds/breaks/aches.

Tap tap tap.

"Christ!" I jump, whip around, tug off my headphones.

"Hey, hey, it's me. It's just me." Lee with his hand on my shoulder.

"Hi, sorry, hi." I turn back to the monitor and quickly sign out of my session.

"What're you doing?"

"Nothing. Email."

We kiss. Lee pulls back, making a face. "Have you been smoking?"

"I—" *Crap.* "Barely. One drag, I *had* to. Margaret had cloves."

"It's shitty for you."

"Right, I know. One drag, Lee, that's all."

"Walk me to chem?"

We walk for a bit, and he doesn't try to touch me, but he's staring, so I go, "Something up?"

"Your face looks different."

"My *face*?"

"I dunno, your eyes, maybe? Is that it? They're darker?"

"No, it's nothing." I shake my head, yanking at my tights and sweater—a far cry from my usual uniform: Lee's old jeans matched with whichever thrift store top is clean. "I lined them, that's all. You've seen them this way before."

He considers me. "I like it." He's nodding now. "It suits you."

51

14.

I get off the bus at Benton and drop into a pocket of hot, sweet air blowing out the kitchen vent of a Mexican bakery. I stop in, buy a big pink cookie and a Coke (old Dakota ritual), then glance out the window. The hill to D's house is twisty and steep. A long residential road that intersects with the eastern stretch of Sunset Boulevard.

Shoving half the cookie in my mouth, I exit the shop. To my left: two Korean markets, a clothing co-op, and a fruit juice stand. To my right: a ninety-nine-cent store. I finish my treat, dust my fingers on my tights, then start the climb.

When I reach the top, I'm breathless and hunched over, hands on knees, staring. There it is: two stories, pink, flat roof, clay tile. I'm dizzy with kid memories: sleepovers, prank calls, brownie binges, dance numbers. I try to see inside, but the house looks dead. Where's Emmett? Do I do this? Do I dare ring the bell?

Slam.

I whip around. It's Julian Boyd, walking away from a battered blue Datsun. "What're you doing here?" he asks, incredulous, as if he's just discovered me hiding at the bottom of his laundry hamper.

"I—what am *I* doing here?" I'm sweaty from the climb and suddenly embarrassed. I pull my sweater away from my tacky body. "Why are *you* here?"

His chest deflates. He looks past me, at the house. "Don't know."

We're quiet. My eyes dart between the car and his face. The car, clearly not a VW Bug. I turn so we're standing side by side, our faces forward. I say, "I'm Adrienne Knox."

"I know who you are."

An unexpected kick, *he knows me*. I look down at my feet, tangled up in an overgrown mess of crispy lawn. "Anyone home?" I ask.

Julian unwraps a single slice of foiled gum. "No," he says, not offering me any. "No one's home."

For dinner, Sam makes spaghetti Bolognese with ground turkey instead of beef. We line our bowls up—one, two, three—on the mosaic coffee table in the den. We curl up in love seats. We twirl pasta and watch the six o'clock news. Sam kisses Mom. I feel cozy and—not happy exactly, but almost-happy, because for three seconds I'm able to forget Dakota. And heartbroken Julian Boyd. I'm home safe. Sam's Bolognese rocks. Mom looks flushed and pretty. But then straight from the sky falls this shitty commotion:

"Turn it up!" Sam's screaming. Mom's kneeling in front of the TV screen, pumping the volume.

"Early this morning, a body, believed to be that of missing fifteen-year-old Cassidy Chang, was discovered along the shoreline not far from the Santa Monica Pier. The Los Angeles teen disappeared late last month after an argument with a family member. Amber King reports."

My head swings to Sam, who looks super stiff and alert. My legs tingle. Then back to school photos of Cassidy as they flash across the screen. She's wearing stripes. She's grinning. More talk of suicide. Of dental records. Another photo: cheek to cheek with a fluffy puppy.

"This past week, another local teen, Dakota Webb—member of the popular SoCal band Dark Star—went missing. Her abandoned Jeep was found in the same beach parking lot where Chang's Ford sedan was discovered late last month. Police are investigating a possible connection."

Mom quickly switches stations. She lands on an insipid sitcom rerun with a laugh track that strikes me as mocking and dark. She grabs my chin with her free hand. "This doesn't mean anything."

The pit in my belly deepens. Any momentary peace I thought I'd found has now completely vanished.

"Nothing's changed," Sam insists.

"I know that," I bluff. I look back at the TV.

15.

The waiting room is windowless. There's a side table made of fake wood, a minifridge, a coffeemaker, and a faux-silver serving platter with stacks of powdered creamer and saccharin packets.

"Ms. Knox."

Officer Walsh shakes my hand and leads me through a cubicle labyrinth to a messy desk by a wall of filmy windows. "Have a seat." He rolls a chair my way, sits with a heavy thud. "Thanks for coming in." He's a big guy. Round and happy-looking with wild, watery eyes.

"Sure."

"Your stepdad—"

"Sam. He's not—he's my mom's boyfriend," I stammer.

"Sorry." He's smacking his clipboard with an eraser head. "Sam said he saw Dakota a few nights before her car turned up. Fighting with someone outside a music venue—" He checks his notes. "The Echo? On Sunset?"

"Yeah."

"Is that a club you frequent?"

"Can't get in." I raise one limp hand. "Seventeen."

Walsh nods. "You know anyone who drives an old Volkswagen like the one Sam saw?"

"No."

"You know anyone who might want to harm Dakota?"

Another "no," followed by a huge dagger of fear jabbing at my solar plexus. My head jumps to Julian. I chew my cheeks out of guilt.

"Were you two close?"

"I—for a while. We're not now." I wait for more. Nothing comes. "Is she—are you sure she's . . . ?" Can't say it. *Is she gone for real, for good, forever?* "What I mean, is—"

"I know what you mean." A beat. "We're exploring every angle."

I tug the loose end of one braid. "She does this, though, you know. Takes off sometimes?"

"Yeah?"

"We were thirteen, maybe? She just—she went away one night. We had plans and she never showed." I shrug. "She turned up, though. Totally fine. She'd, like, spent the night walking. She walked from Echo Park to Sunset Strip and back. She just—she wanted to see if she could do it." I pull a piece of berry gum from my purse, tear off the wrapping, and eat it.

"She did that more than once?"

"Yeah. You stop worrying after a while." I instantly, inexplicably, want to weep.

"When's the last time you two talked?"

"Two years?"

"And you just—grew apart?"

No. "Sort of." No slow drift. We were inseparable and then we weren't.

"Any idea why she reached out to you?" He waits, his face frozen and unreadable. I shake my head as he shifts his weight, uncrossing then recrossing his legs. "Well, what's she like?"

Loves Bowie, Blondie, Red Vines, and brownie batter. Sleeps with a night-light. Loves old horror (*The Exorcist*, *Suspiria*, *The Omen*) and the *West Side Story* movie sound track. "Um, I don't—it's been a while, you know?"

"That's okay." He drops his clipboard. "Did she have anyone special? A boyfriend?"

"I—" I freeze up.

"Okay, you know what?" He waves a hand dismissively, as if to say, *none of this matters*, when we both know that's not true. "What about her band?" He checks his notes. "David Gibbons, Julian Boyd, Gian Colangelo? Know any of them?"

No, yes, no. "Julian." I nod. "I don't know him well. He's in my lit class."

"Do you know if he and Dakota were involved? Romantically? Sexually?"

Yes and yes. "I don't—I just—I don't know that much about him. Or their relationship, really . . ."

"Okay." His smile droops. Then, "It's okay, Adrienne. You're doing great."

This freaks me out. "Oh yeah?" I look down.

"Yes." And after a beat: "Anything else? Something you can think of that might help us find your friend faster?"

I keep my head down. "Sorry," I say.

"Okay, well." Walsh gets up. "You've been helpful."

"Have I?"

16.

Alice Reed is naked, her knees tucked to her concave chest.

"Get in! Fuck, it's freezing, feels great!" Teddy says this, screaming and splashing and clinging to the pool's edge. Lee cannonballs off a large rock. Kate wiggles out of her dinner dress and does an elegant side dive into the deep end. Everyone's drunk. I'm dressed, halfway sober, sitting on a patio chair nursing a small glass of limoncello.

"Adrienne Knox." Kate swims up. Puckers her painted lips. Spits water at my feet. "Get naked, get in."

"No."

"Yes." And when I don't disrobe: "Prude."

She's gone. Lee waves; I salute. Alice giggles, geisha-style, covering two breasts with one hand and whipping water at Lee with the other. I can see one of her nipples. Lee dunks her head underwater. Everyone laughs but me.

"Knox, pass me my drink, will you?"

There are five unmarked cups of Chianti on the patio. I get up, grab one, and pass it to Margaret Yates.

"Thanks." She downs it, facing Teddy. "Okay, I'm ready."

He kisses her, like couples kiss. They do this sometimes. Get drunk and screw around. Teddy likes boys but hasn't been with any yet.

"Again." Margaret whispers, her nose grazing Teddy's. I'm back on my chair but can still read her lips. "Keep going, okay?" She puts his hands on her huge boobs. She loves him. She has zero interest in clothes but lets Teddy dress her like a doll for dinners.

"Stare much?" It's Lee, one wet limb reaching out of the water. He's playfully batting my bare feet.

"I like to watch," I say. "Flirt much?"

"You're not serious." He pushes out of the pool and onto the patio.

"You look so cute together."

"Knox, seriously?" He's smiling, shaking water from his ear. "You're jealous?"

Alice is doing water acrobatics in the shallow end. She does a back flip, flashing a skinny patch of peach pubic hair. "Not really," I say, a little let down by my own apathy.

"Take off your clothes." He grabs at me with icy fingers.

"Put yours back on." I toss a towel over his crotch.

"Why aren't you swimming?"

"Big dinner. Might drown." Do I stay? Go? Being home

feels the same as being here. Crummy. "Have you tried Molly's limoncello?" Molly: Kate's mom.

"Gimme some." He takes my glass and guzzles what's left.

"It's not Jäger," I say, annoyed, grabbing it back. "You're supposed to sip it."

He winces, grinning. Then he gets up, lobs me with his towel, and does a running leap back into the night.

17.

Lit. Murphy's back. He doesn't look any different—glowy or proud or more like a parent. He looks like he's always looked: messy, exhausted, a little lopsided, preppy. Babies should change you, right? Make you seem more mature, more legit or, like, brighten your complexion?

"Essays..." He's walking up my aisle now, dropping papers on desks. I look quickly at Julian, who's looking back, impassively, while fondling the corners of his three-ring binder.

"Stick around after class, please?" Murphy says this. He's talking low and knocking the back of my chair with his wedding ring.

"Will do," I say, darting my eyes back to Julian. Has he talked to anyone yet? Officer Walsh? He looks a little green. Is that guilt? Gloominess? His head is down, so I look away at the wall, not sure what I was expecting to leach out of three seconds of lingering eye contact.

• • •

"I know," I say to Murphy moments later, without prompting.

"So where is it?" he asks, kicking the seat of an empty institutional chair. My essay, he means. "Sit."

"I'm sorry."

"Don't apologize, just turn your work in on time."

"No, I know. I've been a little—I'm not—" I stop, start again: "I'm preoccupied."

His face darkens. He kicks the chair again. "Sit."

I sit. I look down at Murphy's loafers, which are splattered with something yellow and thin. Baby formula? Baby vomit? "You had a baby," I whisper, mindlessly.

He laughs. "I did."

I slap a hand over my mouth, mortified. "Sorry . . . Jesus."

"No, no—no apologies. I had a baby, yeah. A girl, Adeline."

"Sweet name." I drop my hand, straightening up. "Congrats."

"Thanks." His expression settles into something earnest. "Adrienne."

"Hmm?"

"This isn't you."

"What?"

"You've never not turned in work."

I touch my chest as if to say, *Me?* So silly and insincere. Not sure why I do it.

"If you need to talk to someone . . ."

"I don't need to talk to anyone." Then, "That sounded shitty—I—*shit*." Another hand over my mouth. "Sorry. Sorry about the swearing . . ."

He waves it off, leaning back.

"I'm okay, I just—I need an extension. On the essay."

"Okay. So . . . what are we talking? Another week?"

I nod, shrug, push my luck: "Or, like, a week and a half?"

"Get up," he says.

I get up.

"Okay." We shake on it. "So . . . a week and a half from today is . . . what?"

"Monday? I mean, not this Monday, but the following Monday? . . . ish?"

"A week from Monday. The . . ." He's doing the math in his head. "Seventeenth? Don't quote me on that."

I smile, thanking him breathlessly, heading for the exit.

"Adrienne."

I stop. "Yeah?"

"Do me a favor? Just—check in with your counselor? Please?"

I wave one hand high, as if to say, *sure, absolutely*, but I give him no verbal commitment.

18.

Me, Lee, and Kate are at some massive party off Mulholland, just above Runyon Canyon. I don't know whose house this is, but it's big and beige: blank walls, cream-colored carpet, vertical blinds.

"Happy!" Kate screams, shaking my shoulders, smiling psychotically. "Be a happy little bunny!"

I laugh. Kate's crazy. Lee's elsewhere fetching drinks. "Trying," I say, and really, I am. I want to like my life. I want to like my friends, *myself*.

"Know what you need?"

I tilt my head sideways. Kate leans forward and plants a small, soft kiss on my cheek. Tickles. "Cute, right? Tiny kisses. My new move."

"Totes. Super cute."

Then: "What're you wearing?"

I look down. Long, black jersey knit. "New dress."

"So serious," she says, wiggling one eyebrow. "Weren't you having, like, a Francophile moment just last week? Baguettes, berets, Frenchy tunes?"

"I was."

"And this?"

"Goth light."

She wrinkles her nose.

"That was a joke."

She settles against the white wall, taking a long sip off her gnarly Sprite bottle. "Wyatt's here, you know."

"You don't say."

"I do," she says, her mouth splitting into a wide grin. "I say."

I lean back too, browsing the crowd. Some Langley kids, a few from Hollywood High, but most of the faces are fresh to me. "Oh, look," I say, extra dry, taunting Kate. I point left, at Wyatt's head, skimming just above the crowd. "The devil."

She stiffens and pats down her hair. "I look okay?"

"Yes, you're perfect."

"I was thinking I might tell him about when you and I got that nice bread from Gelson's and ate it with those baby cornichons and that blue cheese you like with the thick crust?" I wait for the punch line. She talks on. "'Member? It was super delicious. Like, last month? We made a picnic and put on red lipstick and played Chet Baker on my laptop and ate on your lawn?"

"What the hell are you talking about?"

"You don't remember?"

"Yes, I remember, of course I remember. Why would you tell him that?"

She shrinks. "I like the way it sounds. You don't like the way it sounds? Like we're glamorous? Like we do glamorous things together?"

I laugh. "No, I do, I *do* like it. You're right, sounds sensational."

The smirk returns. She's contented. "You okay if I go?"

"Fine," I say. "I'll find Lee."

She pinches my waist. "I'm gonna go make him make out with me."

"Good"—she's gone before I can get the rest out—"luck." I pull a warm piece of strawberry gum from my pocket, squish it between two fingers, then eat it. I wander away from the wall and end up by the bar, where I see Lee drinking drinks with Alice Reed. I go upstairs. More people, more vertical blinds. I slip sideways through a cracked bedroom door, past some sliding glass, and I'm outside, finally, breathing dry air that smells woody and clean, like night.

I love balconies. I want one. I feel like Juliet for an instant, super moony and romantic. I push forward, tipping myself carefully over the balcony lip. Who would do this? Toss themselves off a building or cliff or into the icy Pacific? What could possibly be that bad?

I pull back and rest my elbows against the cool, rough stucco. The city looks storybookish: dark valleys, squiggly freeways, glittery lights. I lower my gaze to the green, shiny treetops, then lower still, to the street below. A coyote. An angel's trumpet tree. And there, parked four feet from the party: a yellow VW Bug.

I go cold. For a second I just stand there treading water, my heart spazzing out. Moments later, I'm on the street, my nose pressed to the VW's curved back window. There's nothing inside—no candy wrappers, gym sneakers, cigarettes. Nothing that might link the car to its owner. I look back at the house. Whoever's car this is must be inside, right?

Back inside, too many faces. Who am I looking for? A guy? A girl? Someone who seems Dakotaesque? Pretty and pale and lit?

Kate: "Hi, hi, hi." She's tipsy and giddy and grabbing my sleeves. "Where've you been? I've been looking everywhere. Wyatt's with a girl—"

"There's a Bug out front."

"A what?" She's making a face—annoyed she's been cut off. "Where've you been?"

"A yellow *Bug*, Katie. The car Sam saw. Should we go check the plates?" I turn, heading back toward the door.

She grabs at me. "Adrienne. You're freaking me out." Then, soberly: "Seriously. Do you know how many Bugs there are in Southern California?"

"I—" I start to say something sensible—*it's a lead, a clue, it's all we really have*—

She holds her hand up. "Please relax. *Please?* Forget her? For three seconds, just, like, forget she ever existed? Here." She thrusts her cup forward. "Drink something."

"I can't."

"Sure you can. It's sweet, you'll like it."

"No, I can't—" My eyes water. "I can't forget her."

Her shoulders droop. "Okay. Okay, this car. You know it might lead nowhere, right?"

"Why?"

"It's not—*Adrienne*." She frowns. "There are, like, four Bugs that are permanently parked on Sycamore. Four. One has a boot."

Not getting it: "Are they yellow?"

"No, Knox, I just mean"—she grips my shoulders—"you're obsessing over a car. A *car*. This isn't about a car."

"I know it's not about a car."

"It's not really about Dakota, either."

"What do you mean? It *is*. Of course it is."

She shakes her head. "That girl is selfish, Adrienne. You know, you're here, freaking the fuck out, and she's either dead somewhere or alive and warm in the arms of some douchey drug dealer. Either way, *she* did this. She chose this. There's nothing you need to sort out. Finding her, jamming all these jagged, arbitrary puzzle pieces into place, won't get you any closer to understanding why she shit all over you and your friendship." She stops. Inhales. "You all right?" she asks. "You look bad." A funny beat while she inspects my face. "You wanna go or no?"

Out of me comes a very small whimper. I wipe my eyes, feeling hopelessly frustrated. "I'm just—I'm sorry," I say, confused and super spent. "I don't know what I want."

19.

I'm on my bedroom floor with the computer in my lap, smoking my third consecutive cigarette. I'm rewatching the Dakota/Dark Star video. It's those same loopy sounds again, only this time I notice the dancing: how she rocks gently to her own fluttery voice—pretty, unassuming, swishy movements. This kills me. Why? Because on her—the dancing and dim lights—it all looks so easy and right. Why wasn't *I* born this way? Effortlessly cool?

I hit replay. I can't even remember the real Dakota. This—this pretty package—is this who she was/is? Is this who I am? An adoring fan?

New search: "Dakota Webb missing." A gazillion links flash in my face. I click one that leads to some music forum with pages of speculation about her disappearance. Suicide, murder, kidnappings, claims of scientology involvement, conspiracy theories, a handful of kids from Langley reminiscing about the last time they saw her alive (at a Smell show, at Grauman's Chinese, at a deli on third, snorting things in public restrooms).

Knock, knock.

. I jump, startled shitless, smooshing my cigarette tip into a plate and fanning the air. "Who's there?"

"It's me," comes a drunk, familiar boy voice.

I undo the door a crack. "What're you doing here, Lee? It's late."

His face is splotchy from drinking. "You left the party and didn't say good-bye. Door was open . . ." He pushes in, grabbing my cheeks and kissing me. "*Fuck*," he whines, shoving me lightly. "Fuck, *Adrienne*—" He's laughing now. "What's with the cigarettes all of a sudden?"

"What's the big deal?" I squeal, sounding psychotically defensive. "Why do you care? It's not *your* body."

"It kind of is . . ." Lee says, clutching my hips. "And anyways, I'm the one who has to kiss you."

I turn away, embarrassed. "It's just a thing, okay? I'll stop soon."

He wraps his arms around my waist. His nose grazes my neck. "Where'd you go tonight?"

My body kick-starts—a low buzzing that starts in my knees and moves upward. "Nowhere," I whisper. "I'm right here."

He kisses me. This time, I kiss back. One of his hands is clamped around the back of my head, the other is lifting my dress up. "I like this," he says, backing me into my blue bed-room wall. "This black thing. It's sexy."

Something angry and hot slips down my spine. *I'm not dressed like me.* "It's not," I say, my voice sounding sharp.

"It is," he insists, undoing the clasp at my breastbone. Then, "Adrienne, hey, look at me." I glance up. His eyes are pink and glassy. "You're beautiful," he says, plainly. And inexplicably—*so quick*—Lee slides out of place in my heart.

20.

Kate passes me a big bag of wasabi chips. "Want some?"

I take two and chew, feeling mildly high while the spiciness eats at my sinuses. "Where're we going?"

"Don't know. Sandwiches? Or we could get takeout from that vegan place on La Cienega? You liked their lentil salad. 'Member?"

I nod. We're weaving through the student lot, headed for Kate's car.

"Get that, will you?" She's searching her bag for her keys. Something's tacked to the grimy windshield. I stretch across the hood and pry the paper loose from under the wiper.

Dark Star performs a Dakota Webb tribute show.
Thursday night, 8 p.m., the Smell

My balance seesaws. It's a black-and-white Xeroxed photo of Dakota in her room. She's laughing and looking sideways. Who took this? Julian?

"What is it?" Kate calls from inside the car.

"Nothing," I say, pocketing the flyer and getting in. "Trash."

21.

I'm wearing beat-to-shit booties and kicking around outside the Smell. There's a loud, smoky pack of girls huddled together by the club entrance looking ratty and elfin and chic. I dig my phone from my purse and shakily dial Dakota. Straight to voicemail, of course. I flip my phone shut.

Inside it's all brick walls and cement flooring. A gazillion Langley kids hold candles and lighters. Girls with Kool-Aid-colored hair sip things encased in brown baggies. Is this what I've been missing? Dank rooms and cuckoo crowds?

Dark Star is midway through their set, playing an instrumental version of my favorite—"Art School Sluts with Razored Haircuts." I'm used to the scratchy acoustic version they have up on their website. Without Dakota, the song's spoiled.

I box through the swaying masses and end up near the front by the stage. This blond girl from my civics class is whispering lyrics. Julian's up onstage pounding the shit out of a monster drum set. There's an empty mic stand where Dakota used to be.

Then: show's over. Everyone goes outside to smoke. I stay, watching the band pack up their equipment. Julian— he knows something, he does, he *must*. Could he have hurt her? Smothered her? Sent her running? Broken her? No way, right? That's Dakota's game. She does the breaking.

Julian sees me and hops off the stage. I wave, but he keeps on toward the exit.

"Hey," I say, impulsively, grabbing at him. "Hey, wait. Please?" He stops. Stares at my fingers clutching his hot arm. I get a fast flash of him and Dakota doing indecent things together. "That was great," I babble, trying to make the moment feel more upbeat and normal. "You were great," I say, pulling my hand back, flustered.

"Thanks."

"I kind of—I was hoping to talk to you."

"I—we have to load up the van."

"Oh." I shrug. "That's okay. I'll see you tomorrow," I blather, mortified. Why am I standing here, begging a stranger for time and attention?

"Just—" He looks up. "Wait, if you want. We'll be done in fifteen."

"Oh."

"There's a place next door that'll serve us."

I unclench my fists.

"Wait here, okay?" He's jogging backward now.

"Okay." I nod casually. "Cool."

The backs of my thighs are glued to the sticky black bar booth. Ranchera music pumps out of a large speaker by the window. Julian drops two Negra Modelos onto the tabletop. "Here."

I take a timid sip of beer and try not to stare as he chugs half his bottle, still standing. "You come here a lot?" I ask.

He swallows. "When we're downtown, I guess. After shows." He sits, finally, slumping against the booth back.

"You guys, you're getting pretty big, huh?" Underground following. Weekly Smell shows. Rumor of indie label interest. Of summertime West Coast tour plans.

"We were on the verge." Julian half laughs. Of course, *Christ*, what's a band without their lead girl? *Stupid, stupid, stupid, Adrienne.* "We're not really sure what we're doing anymore."

"Sorry."

He shakes a shoulder. One careless wiggle.

"So, tonight . . ." I say, sounding inane. Where am I headed with this—*Great tribute? Super moving?*

"She never talked about you," Julian blurts. My neck tenses. He looks sorry he said it. "I don't mean—I mean, I knew you two were friends, like, forever ago, I just—she never talked about it."

79

"Oh."

"So. What happened?" He's rubbing his beard scruff. "Why'd you two stop—"

"No reason," I say, cutting him off. "Girl stuff, I guess." I shift around in my seat, my thighs making puckering sounds as they pull away from the pleather. "Sam saw her."

"Sorry?"

"No, I mean—not, like, recently. I mean the weekend she . . ." I trail off, wondering what he's thinking. Why his face looks so infuriatingly blank.

"Who's Sam?"

"Oh." *Jesus.* "My mom's boyfriend?" I suck back more beer. Make it look like I like it. "She was outside the Echo." I watch his face for flickers of recognition. "In a Bug."

"A Bug?"

"Yeah, you know, the car?"

He nods. "Want another?"

"Still have to finish this one."

He's already at the bar buying two more. "Here." He sits back down and slides one my way. "So, she was with someone?"

Can't stop myself: "Wasn't you?"

He swallows. "Wasn't me." He's gazing intently at his beer bottle. He looks jilted. Heartsick.

I backpedal. "I don't know if it was a guy. Could've been a girl. Sam didn't see . . ."

He guzzles his drink, stares at the back of the bar, undoes the clasp on his wristwatch.

"Here. You should hear this." I pull my cell from my bag. Dial voicemail. Punch in my password. Pass him the phone. Dakota's small voice—tinny and far away—seeps from the cell speaker: "Adrienne? Adrienne, it's me, remember? Call back, please?"

All the color leaks from his cheeks. "When was this?"

"A few days before."

"Can I hear it again?"

"Press four."

He does. He listens. He passes the phone back. "Did you call back?"

"No." Shame on me. "Was she your girlfriend?" I ask, cautiously, after sixty seconds of wearisome silence. "I mean, I know you guys were involved, but . . . were you together? Like, officially?"

"That girl—" He smiles tightly. "Never really belonged to anyone."

"Sorry, you're just—" I'm grinning. "You're really right." For an instant I feel less alone. "So she wasn't . . . ? I mean, I always thought you were a couple."

"Sometimes," he says, hesitating a second. "Sometimes not." He peels the label off his bottle.

22.

"Where were you last night?" asks Lee, his palm flat against my lower back.

I arch away, leaning into my locker. "Home." I trade my trig text for *Frankenstein*.

"I called you."

"I know."

"You didn't pick up."

Second bell. I lock my locker and spin on one heel, slipping past Lee and down the hall.

"Hey." He's at my side now, running to keep up. "What's your problem?"

A quick flash of guilt. "Nothing." I stop, facing him. "I'm just late for class."

"Well, so am I."

"Okay," I say, softening. "Sorry."

"So kiss me."

I hesitate for a second, then roll up onto my tippytoes. I peck his lips.

"That's it?"

"*Lee.*" I pull away, wiping my mouth. "I'm late."

"Fine," he says. His voice is clipped. "So go."

After lit, Murphy packs up his crap. Kids scatter. Julian looms over my desk.

I get up, bite my pen tip, grab my bag, and together we go outside. Just like that. No talking, no sad glances—we walk quickly, side by side, off campus to the freak section. Julian sits on a slab of cement and lights two skinny cigarettes. He passes me one. I drag deeply, looking up, batting my eyes at Kate's tall, glossy palm trees. Something brushes against my elbow. I look down. It's Julian's arm. I can't tell if he's touching me on purpose or not. I stay still. I like him there, his army jacket rubbing against my dress sleeve.

"Time's up." Second bell blares. "See ya," he says, standing, leaving me. Snuffing out his cigarette and walking away without turning back.

"Have you seen that thing he's dating?"

"That *thing*?" I ask, cranking the window down, hot exhaust pelting my face. "Yes, I've seen her. She's cute."

Kate accelerates, speeding through a yellow light. "*Cute?* She's tiny. She's like—" She makes a sour face. "Like a shrunken, emaciated doll. Who would have sex with that?"

"Wyatt. Apparently."

"Fuck you."

I laugh.

"No, *fuck you*. Why can't you be my friend and hate her with some commitment and sincerity?"

"I'm sorry."

"Are you?"

"Yes!"

"You're still laughing!"

"Yes! *Yes*, sorry," I say, turning up the enthusiasm. "She's a troll."

Kate eases up on the gas. "I'm better than her."

"Katie . . . *hey*." I rub her shoulder. "Yes. Come on, you're my favorite person." Her shoulders slump. "No one else brings me tiny, delicious snacks from the Japanese market or buys me books about controversial but revolutionary treatments in the fight against anorexia nervosa."

She laughs.

"And you have the prettiest red lips."

"Makeup."

"And you have the best taste in experimental jazz."

"True . . ."

"And does that girl Wyatt's with take bubble baths *every single day*? Does she line dry her clothes like you do?"

A modest shrug.

"You're a movie star."

My cell dings. I grab my bag, fishing my phone from the side compartment and checking the ID screen. "Huh."

"What?"

"Number's blocked."

"So?" Kate makes a circular gesture with her hand. "Answer it."

"I—" I pick up. "Hello?" Zilch. Silence. Then, again: "Hello?" The line clicks dead.

"What? Who was it?"

"I—no one?" I roll the window up, feeling suddenly, inexplicably chilly. "I dunno. No one was there."

23.

"I wanna know who you love best."

"You already know who I like best."

"Not like, love." Her mouth goes taut. "Seriously. Your favorite. Who's the person you love more than anyone else in the world?"

"Excluding my mother?"

"Obviously."

We both smile. "Hmm . . ." I stretch the moment. For once, making her wait for it. "You?"

So pleased: "Me?"

"Yes, you," I say, eyes rolling. "You're ridiculous."

She winks, turning back to her reflection. Then she bee-lines for my closet, pulling three dresses off the rack and tossing them onto my bedspread.

"Feel free . . ."

She strips down, flinging her shirt, shoes, shorts, and bra

onto my floor. "You think I look fat?" She's just standing there. Naked, save for her striped cotton underwear.

"No." My eyes dart nervously to the cracked bedroom door. Sam's home.

"You're not even looking."

I glance up. "You're not fat, no." She knows this. She's tiny and pale with perfect, perky little boobs that match.

"Shit." Now she's all twisted up, struggling to get one of the dresses over her head. "Success!" Once on, watching herself: "It's see-through."

"That's the style." Sheer floral. "It goes with a slip."

She scowls. Strips down again. Tries another. My vintage navy shift. "Can I wear this?" She's inspecting herself sideways in the full-length. She looks spectacular. Like a sixties school-girl pinup.

"Where?"

"On my date."

Typical secret, cagy bullshit. "Who are you dating?"

No response. Instead: "Sometimes I think—" She starts, then stops, hurling herself down onto the floor, next to me. "Don't you ever wonder what real love feels like?"

I tell her everything. Every kiss, crush, grope. "Real love?"

"Yeah. Like really real love."

"I guess," I say, uneasy. "Sure." I pick at the berber carpet, pulling loose a few nylon loops.

"I never think about loving anyone. You think that's weird?"

"I—" I stiffen. "Never?"

"Not ever." She blinks. "I only ever think about people loving me."

I look at her perfect, poreless complexion. Her bony shoulders. Her puffy upper lip. "That dress looks better on you," I say.

She pulls her chin to her chest, looking down, assessing herself. "Does it?" she asks.

"Yes," I say. "It does."

24.

It's five thirty. I'm in bed with *Jane Eyre*.

"How's the essay coming?" Lee says this. He's behind me, nudging my butt with his knee. I'm fake reading and staring out the window at the neon pink-blue sky. "Your *essay*?" he says again, when I don't respond.

I wave *Jane* overhead. "Can't write the thing until I read the book."

"Wasn't it due this week?" Another knee nudge.

"Monday, yes." I reach around and grab his shin, shoving him off me. "And can you shut up so I can get through this?"

Lee stiffens. I get that tight, shitty feeling in my neck. I try reinvesting in the book, but I am blazingly, psychotically pissed. I hate him. *Why* do I hate him? He does nothing but coddle and care for me, and I'm an absolute dick back.

"Adrienne." He sounds pathetically low.

"I'm sorry," I say quickly, feeling sudden regret and shame.

"Come'ere, please?"

He's begging. So I roll over and let him kiss me. I even like the way it feels: warm, familiar. He touches my hair, my hands, my lopsided boobs. Then he reaches beneath my skirt. "Don't," I say, no longer liking it.

"Why not?"

He tries again, so I clamp his hand between my thighs. "Lee." My breath catches. "Stop it. I don't want to."

He glares at me, his eyes wounded and wet. Then he's up off the bed and into the bathroom.

I wince and tug my skirt down, rolling back onto my side.

25.

"Gimme the bread."

"Gimme?" Kate mimics, grabbing the bread basket, holding it high off the table. "Say, 'May I.'"

Teddy's drunk. He slurs, "May I."

"May I what?"

They're locked in a playful stare-off. "The bread. Gimme."

She rolls her eyes and drops the basket. Leans into me. Whispers: "You and Lee look so cozy over there."

Lee's across the table serving Alice piles of puffy salad.

"That's not me."

"No way," she deadpans, pulling back. "Hey, Lee," she shouts. "Go get more wine. There're two reds by the microwave."

He gets up. Kate faces me. "Put a leash on that guy." She shoves a forkful of pasta into her mouth, then turns to Margaret Yates, who goes, "Guess what?"

"What?"

"A freshman from Hollywood High tried to drown herself at Venice Beach today."

"This *afternoon*?" Kate shrieks.

"Broad daylight. She's fine. Lifeguard on duty. She got saved."

Lee's back with both bottles. "What happened?"

"Nothing." Kate waves him forward with one hand. "Wine, please."

I exhale, relieved no one's dead, but then:

"I saw two cops with Julian Boyd by the faculty lot after school." Alice says this. Contributing something of substance for once.

"Doing what?" Teddy asks.

"Talking. I dunno. You think that's weird?"

"Not weird," I blurt. "They're talking to everyone. They talked to me."

Shit stops. Records screech. All eyes on me.

"You talked to the police?" Margaret asks, her brow creasing.

"She knew her, that's all." Lee to my defense. "No big deal." He looks at me.

"Yeah, I just, I knew her," I stammer.

"How?" Teddy asks.

"We were friends for a while. Before I met you guys."

"You never mentioned it."

"Didn't I?"

"No," Margaret says, watching me like I'm someone she's met before but whose name she can't remember. "Were you close?"

I shrug.

"But"—her eyes dart down my body—"you're not like her."

"What's that supposed to mean?"

"Like, I dunno, you're not *crazy*."

"Knox?" Kate quips, trying to lighten the mood. "Knox is nuts. Absolutely *wild*." She uncorks one of the reds and waves the bottle around. "Want more?"

Teddy thrusts his cup forward and the energy lifts a little.

"Well, whatever," Margaret says, talking on. "I like Julian Boyd. He's a babe." She shoves Teddy sideways. "He'll make a good suspect."

Ice-cold, I say, "Suspect?"

"Sure, why not? This whole thing is already a huge fucking soap opera. Now there's some homeless dude who's claiming he saw Dakota the night she disappeared, like, *walking* into the water. But then Teddy knows a guy—" She faces him. "What's his name again?"

"Nate Garza."

"Right, who says Julian has this wicked jealous streak, and that no way in hell would she kill herself—"

"But then, who knows, right?" Teddy again. "Because I

also heard she had a Klonopin habit. And that stuff is—it's antianxiety, right? Or antidepression?"

"Hey, guys?" I warble, on the verge of implosion.

Kate puts her hand on my neck. She shakes her head, says, "Stop it."

"Stop *what*?"

"Are you deaf? Did you not hear her say they were friends?"

Margaret's mouth tightens. "I—" She starts to say something cute, then, "Sorry." She's facing me now. "Didn't mean to offend."

26.

Kate leads me through a crowd of fourteen-year-old girls in Stetsons and sundresses fingering ten-dollar necklaces. We do this most Sundays. Melrose Trading Post at Fairfax High. Used paperbacks, used furniture, white lace shirts with yellow pit stains.

"Eat this," Kate says, passing me the last of a Nutella crepe. "And come'ere." She pulls me into a cluttered booth. Pulls a minishift off the rack. "I like the print. Try it on."

Faded mint polka dot. Pretty, but I have zero zeal for shopping. "Why don't *you* try it on?"

"Green makes me look sallow." She stares at me for a few seconds, then puts the dress back. "You ever gonna pep up?"

No clue. I take a bite of crepe and trash the rest. We're walking again. I spot a woman selling clothes arranged by color. I go for the blacks and blues. "What do you think of this?" I ask, tugging on something knee-length and dark.

"Where're you gonna wear that? Up onstage?"

"Screw you." I turn toward the mirror. "Trying it on." I slip the dress over my shirt. It's tight around my ribs and dips between my boobs. "How much?" I ask the woman manning the booth.

"Fifteen."

"Buying it," I say to Kate, who rolls her eyes. I unzip the back and shimmy out. I pull a five, a ten, from my purse and thank the tiny lady.

"Chiffon. So versatile."

"Shut up." I clutch the dress to my chest and push forward. We hop from booth to booth, browsing. Kate says, "I'm pretty sure Alice likes Lee."

I search inside for signs of jealousy. "I know."

"Do you care?"

"I mean." I pick up a chipped magnifying glass. "I guess? I dunno, doesn't really feel worthy of worry. Alice isn't the most complex girl in the world."

"You just—" She makes a face. "You don't seem very invested in your relationship right now."

A surge of fear, followed by a bleak, tangential thought: Dakota—drugged, beaten, bound, maimed. I shake off the image, redirecting my focus. "I'm invested," I say to Kate. Her brow crinkles. "What? I am. I'm just—I'm not his keeper."

"But you are."

"But I'm not." Would it be so bad if Lee left me? I'd be on my own, absolved of any blame or guilt. "He's a free agent."

"He's not. He's *not* free, Knox, that's the point. He's your *boyfriend*. Why commit to someone you're not interested in being committed to?"

"Who says I'm not?"

She sighs, exasperated.

"Look," I say, eager for new topics. I grab a wool fedora off a hat stand and slap it over her ponytail. "Sweet."

She laughs, despite herself, popping her head in front of a mirror tacked to the side of a van. "I look like those little girls in Stetsons."

"You do," I say, thrusting my new old dress over one shoulder. "You're cute, Katie. It's a good look."

27.

Julian's not in lit, so, like a lunatic, I spend most of Murphy's *Franken*-lecture pushing the panic back by picturing his possible whereabouts: He's home, hungover. His car's stalled out on Beverly. He's behind the school drinking black coffee from a blue paper cup.

"Adrienne."

Why do I care? Who the hell is Julian Boyd anyway? Not a real person. He doesn't have a mom, or go to a pediatric dentist still, like I do. He's a luminary. A myth. He's what's left to gawk at now that Dakota's gone away.

"Adrienne."

I snap to.

"Can we talk?" Murphy, of course. He's next to me now, wedged behind a small square desk, like mine.

"I—okay." I straighten up. Class is over. I've just been sitting here, zoned out like a lobotomized lump.

"*Jane Eyre*."

"Sure." I shake my head. "I'm almost . . ." I don't finish. I have nothing to offer but transparent excuses.

"Not done?"

"Right, not yet."

He rubs his nose with two flat fingers, leaning forward. "Well, have you had a chance to see Griffin?" Guidance.

"I just—" I dodge the question. "I need a little bit more . . . can I have more time? With the essay, I mean."

He's eyeballing me now. "Adrienne, it's not just the essay. You've stopped participating, you've gotten Ds on your past two quizzes . . . you used to be fully invested in discussions." He stops to suck in some air. "You *loved* this class."

I did. "Still do."

"Adrienne." His face says *bullshit*. "*Talk* to me. You're having a tough time. That's an okay thing to say out loud."

I laugh. Like an idiot, petulant, piece-of-shit *kid*.

"Okay, or . . . walk with me."

"Where?"

"Come on, get up. Let's go see Griffin."

My stomach seizes. "I don't need to see Griffin."

He's standing now. "Okay." And shifting back and forth from leg to leg. We watch each other. I wonder briefly what his regular life is like. What he's like at home, with Gwen, their baby. Sweet, I'm guessing. Superattentive, like Lee.

"Just—" He throws one hand up. "Monday, okay? Get me *Jane* by Monday."

See? Such a softy. "Yes." I exhale.

"*Monday*, Adrienne. Seriously." He grabs his leather tote off the back of his chair. "After this, no more favors."

Me, Mom, Sam—at the fish taco stand on Sunset.

"Where's Lee, babe?" Mom shovels a chip into a massive pile of ceviche.

I shrug, say, "Home."

"Everything okay?"

"Fine."

"And Katie?" She chews merrily. "How's she? We haven't seen her since—"

"Sunday," Sam interjects. "'Member? She dropped Adrienne off after the flea market."

"Oh, right." More chewing. More staring. "New dress, babe?"

"Yep."

Her smile looks wobbly and ready to crack. She gets up, rubbing greasy fingers against her jeans. "You guys need anything? Habanero? More salsa?"

"No, thanks." I shove half a taco into my mouth and watch as she swerves toward the condiment bar. "What the fuck," I say to Sam once she's gone.

"Watch your mouth." He knocks my elbow with his soda cup.

"And cut your mother some slack. She's worried about you."

"Worried *why*?"

"Look at you." He wrinkles his nose. "What the hell are you wearing?"

"A dress."

"Clever kid . . ." He taps his temple. Then, "Look, Mom just thought . . ."

Another huge bite. I'm not even done chewing the last. "What? Mom thought what?"

He sniffs. "Are you and Lee okay?"

My mouth is so stuffed I can barely speak. "*Why?*"

"Jesus, Adrienne, eat faster."

I laugh. Don't mean to. But Sam's jokes always hit unexpectedly. I'm choking on fried fish.

"You need the Heimlich?" He's leaning across the table, patting my back while I hack up a lung. "I'm certified."

I swallow finally, clutching my chest, breathless.

"What's so funny?" Mom's back with two tiny containers of pico de gallo. "What? What'd I miss?"

"Some sort of magic," Sam boasts. "I made Morticia laugh."

"*Morticia*?" I screech.

Mom smothers a guilty giggle with one hand and high-fives Sam with the other.

"You both suck," I say, kneeing the table.

They high-five again.

28.

I'm at school superearly, camped out at Julian's favorite smoking spot. I sit, restlessly chewing my cheeks until ten past eight. He's a no-show.

At half past, between first and second bell, I go and wait by his locker like a dumb dog. Kate passes by on her way to trig. She flicks a paper clip at my boob and flashes me a curious smirk, but doesn't stop to say hi.

Ten to nine: I board the city bus.

Fifteen past: I get off at Benton Way.

More cheek chewing. More shitty paranoia. I buy a pink cookie at the Mexican bakery, then I hike the hill to Dakota's house.

He's there. That's him, *he's there*. Blue Datsun. Cigarette. He's on a stakeout. I jog toward the car, elated. Relieved. "Hey," I say, tapping at the passenger-side window.

Julian jumps, exhaling smoke. Then he reaches over and pops the lock.

"What're you doing here?"

I get in. "You're missing lit."

"So are you."

He offers me his cigarette. I take it, dragging on the damp, hot filter. "So you've just . . . been *here* this whole time? Watching the house?"

He shrugs.

"What about school?"

"What about it?"

I pass the cig back. "Well . . . have you seen anything?"

He shifts around. "You think I'm crazy, right? Sitting here? Expecting her to just . . . show up?"

"I don't think you're crazy," I say, and it's true, I don't. I settle against the broken leather headrest, relaxing finally after days of creepy jitters. I pull the cookie from my knapsack.

"Holy shit," Julian croaks.

It's Emmett. *Emmett*, headed toward his Ford sedan with a vinyl computer bag slung over one shoulder. We slump in our seats.

"Can he see us?"

"I don't know," I squeak. "Can he?" He looks so normal: skinny, shaggy, serious, sullen. "What the hell, where's he going?"

"Work?"

"How can he work? How can he work when his kid's missing?"

"Not his kid," Julian says, and he's right. Emmett's the fake parent. Default dad. The guy who took over when Dakota's mom left, long ago.

"There he goes," I say, sitting up. He's off. We watch the car disappear down Mohawk.

We're quiet for a bit. Julian messes with the stereo. I watch Dakota's sad Jeep, parked at an angle in front of the garage, and wonder how long it's been back. How these things work. How long it takes to dust for fingerprints or search for bodily fluids or strands of hair. "Hungry?" I offer, passing him some crumpled cookie.

Dingaling.

"Crap." My cell. I grab at it, thinking it's Griffin in Guidance or maybe Murphy or Kate, wondering where the hell I'm at, but—"Christ"—it's that private number again. I pick up, overeager. "Hello?"

Dead air.

"Hello, hello?"

Another hang-up.

"What?" he says. "What's with your face?"

I must look insane. I *feel* insane—manic, mistrustful—but also, I'm antsy. I can't sit still. I'm just so sick of all this hopelessness. "Let's break in," I suggest.

His mouth clicks open. "What?"

"Come on, let's. Emmett used to keep a spare key inside a fake rock by the back door."

"What do you expect to find? The cops . . . I mean, I'm sure anything good is already gone."

"Well, what do you expect to find sitting *here*?" I push the car door open and climb out. "I'll go on my own." I feel reckless and high. I stalk toward the house. Halfway up the drive, I hear this:

"Adrienne!" It's the first time he's said my name. "Wait, okay? Please, wait? I'm coming, just—gimme a sec."

I spot it instantly. "Fake rocks look so fake." Wedged between the watering can and a strategically placed pile of real rocks. I grab at it, brush off the dirt, and shake out the key. "Voilà."

Julian's face is green.

"You okay?"

No response.

I wiggle the key in the lock. "Open sesame." The door pops.

"You sure you wanna do this?"

Where's his daring dark side? His wild streak? The cool criminal within? "We're not gonna get caught."

"That's not what . . ." He trails off. What's he so scared of? Booby traps? Alarm bells? Dakota's lifeless body? "Okay," he continues, pushing past me. "Let's go, then."

· · ·

It's the dank smell that hits first: musty and stuck. Then something else: something waxy and sweet and warm underneath. Dakota smell. Her perfume, maybe? I clutch the kitchen counter for support.

"You all right?"

This. *This* is what he meant. Did I really want to *smell her?* Or see her wallpapered walls or her bed?

"Come on," Julian says, pulling me forward by the elbow. "Let's go upstairs."

It's been two years since I've been here last, but it all looks exactly the same: mismatched furniture; heavy blinds; clean, dark wood floors. Dakota's room is black and blue, with a four-poster bed, a record player, an electronic keyboard, and a Bowie poster. For a minute or two, Julian and I just stand there. Then he starts searching. He picks through a stack of papers on her bureau, pulls a few books off the shelf.

I'm not even sure what I'm looking for. A Klonopin prescription? A notebook with my name scrawled in the margins? I start under the bed, where all her CDs are stored in big plastic bins. I pull out two discs, look inside, place them back in their jewel cases. I look at Julian. I look at the Bowie poster. I think about my old navy shift dress. The one I loaned Dakota the day I got ditched. I get up and go to the closet.

Racks of silky, witchy dresses, dark linen tops, thin band T-shirts, no navy shift. I touch everything. I dig to the back and tug loose my favorite: sheer black chiffon, similar to the one I bought with Kate at the flea market. Dakota wore this one weekly. I look over my shoulder at Julian. He's got his back to me. He's jiggling a loose floorboard. I quickly shove the dress in my purse (an eye for an eye, a dress for a dress), then mindlessly turn my attention to an army jacket with Sharpie scrawl splattered all over its sleeves.

"Oh, wow." Julian's eyeing the coat. It lies in a ball by my feet.

"What?" I ask, picking it up. "What is it?"

"Her favorite. Lemme see?"

I toss it. He shakes out the wrinkles, holds up both sleeves. "Show dates," he says, proudly, pointing at the sloppy print. "Dark Star dates."

I go and sit beside him on the floor. I stare. That's her handwriting—messy, slanted, small. "You guys played out a lot, huh?" Tons of dates, all arranged in skinny, crooked columns.

"I guess."

I feel spacey, shaky, and worn-out. I think about the dress in my purse and get a quick pang of shame. "Feels weird here."

"Does it?"

"Doesn't it?" I roll my knees to one side. Rest my head

against the purple bed skirt. "She used to get really pissed at me." I flash back to the last time we were here. Dakota and me, shit-show drunk and fighting.

"Over what?"

"Dunno. Everything. She thought I was, like, judgey and smug. That I didn't approve of the things she liked. I used to do stupid stuff to prove I was cool." I laugh to offset my embarrassment.

"Like?"

"Like . . . drink a lot. I dunno. That's what made me think—" I stop, gesturing vaguely around the room. "Last time I was here, we fought."

"About?"

"We were drunk, I don't know."

"Was that the last time . . . ?" He lets the sentence dangle. "I mean, was that when you two stopped . . . ?"

"No, no," I'm quick to say, although it's possible that fight was all part of some larger lead-up. "We still hung out for a while after that." I pause to laugh. "She spit in my face."

"What?"

"She spit ice at me. Right here." I tap the bed. "Ice and schnapps."

Julian snorts. An unexpected, utterly uncool little grunt. "Not surprised. We used to have epic, gnarly, crazy fights. We'd be in the car and she'd be screaming, swearing, skidding sideways off the road, and then she'd stop the Jeep and make me get out. Happened twice, super late. Got to jog home in the dark."

I'm smiling. So is he. He looks down at the jacket. The smiling stops.

"What?"

He's touching two dates. "We haven't—we've only been playing together a year and a half."

"So?"

"So, this date? This was, like, two years ago." He shakes his head, four fast motions. "We hadn't even met yet."

We were friends still.

Julian slides backward, away from the coat.

"It ain't alive," I quip.

No laugh back. I feel idiotic. I rack my brain for explanations. "Maybe she was singing on her own somewhere? Open mics, maybe?"

"Did she play out, back then?"

"I don't—" No? Maybe? "It's possible. She didn't always tell me stuff."

"And, okay—here?" He's pointing at new numbers. "I'd sprained my wrist. Couldn't drum." He smoothes out both sleeves. "These aren't show dates." He looks up, panicked. "She told me they were show dates. Why would she lie about that?"

My belly flops.

"I mean, some of them *are* show dates." He sighs, rolling

the bed sideways. "Jesus, I dunno, ya know?" He's fumbling with the floorboard again. "Help me with this?"

I grab a nail file off the nightstand and use it to jimmy one corner free. A satisfying *pop*. Julian wiggles the board back and forth. The whole thing comes loose. Inside, arranged neatly, a manila envelope folded lengthwise. An old photo of a pretty blonde holding a squirmy child. Three plastic Baggies wrapped tightly with tape and Saran wrap.

"How'd you know?"

"Saw her screwing with it once." He grabs the plastic bags first. Pockets those.

"Hey."

"Candy." He picks up the picture. "Her mother," he says, and on closer inspection I see it: same saucer eyes and wispy hair. Same bird bones and big boobs.

"And baby Dakota?"

"Looks like." He passes the pic and goes for the envelope. Unfolds it. Out slide three shiny sheets of photo paper.

"Proofs."

Dozens of tiny black-and-white images arranged side by side in neat little rows. I squint at a naked blonde rolling around on a bare mattress.

"Wow," Julian croaks.

It's her. She's clutching a comforter. A few of the shots have Xs and checks next to them. A man's name, Mark Mills, is scribbled in blue ink along the side of each sheet. "Photographer?"

"Manager," Julian says, his face contorting.

"Yours?"

"No. Just, this, like, sketch guy that was always sniffing around after shows. He manages another Smell band." Then: "*Christ*. What the hell *is* this? Were they together?"

He's near tears.

"This dude is so sleazy."

My heart pretty much explodes in my chest. "Hey, it's okay," I say, trying to touch him. He flinches. "Why not . . ." I scooch back a bit, giving him room to breathe. "I mean, do you know him? Could you call him? Let's just call the guy and see what he knows."

"No, this dude—" He's looking at me like I'm bat-shit insane. "Adrienne, *no*." He shuffles through the proofs again. "August eighteenth."

"Hmm?"

He points at some tiny lettering beneath the manager's name. "August eighteenth." Then grabs the jacket and points at the same date written on Dakota's coat cuff. "They match."

I pick up the proofs. Look closely. Typed in diminutive print in the margins of each page is *8/18*. "No show that night?"

"No show."

I scan the photos. Where the hell was she? Someone's

bedroom? A loft? The space looks industrial and bare.

Then: one candid shot. Last image. Dakota: nude, no blanket, smoking. Her hips, hollow and pointy. I inhale and catch a whiff of something sad. "Can we go?"

"Right now?"

I sit up. Shove everything back in the envelope. "Yeah, you mind?" And, "Can I keep these?"

"Wait, *why*?"

"Just for a few days. Please? I just—I want to see if there's something we're missing."

He sucks his upper lip. "Fine." Slides the floorboard back into place.

We stand. I scan the room one last time. Why no evidence of Julian, of band mates, of *me*?

"You ready?"

"Yep."

Too typical. Her not needing anyone but needing every-one to need her.

29.

"Shit, Knox, you're blitzed."

True. Drank a quarter of Sam's smoky scotch before I boarded the bus for Kate's place.

"What's in the bag?" she asks, prying the soggy brown sack from my fingertips.

"Blueberry pie."

She peeks inside. "You sit on it?"

I laugh. Kate laughs. Purple filling oozes onto her dry, white hands.

Walker, Yates, and Reed huddle around their supper plates, staring. And Lee? Lee's at my side, peeling my coat off my body, yanking me into the kitchen.

"You're drunk?"

"I'm hungry." I pull myself up onto the sticky countertop. "When do we eat?"

"What the hell happened to you? We *ate* already."

I dig into some leftover congealed artichoke dip with my pinkie. "Yum."

"Knox, look at me." He grabs my chin. "You smell."

"That's the scotch."

"Why are you like this?"

"Like what?"

"Because of *her*?"

"Because of *her*?" I mimic.

Kate appears, carrying a stack of crusty plates. Lee turns, says, "Take care of this?"

Now Kate's in my face with a bowl of cold chicken and roasted beets. "Eat, drunkles." I let her feed me. The beets are sweet and tangy and I swing my legs back and forth while I chew.

30.

I tell Sam I'm sick. He knows I'm hungover. I skip school, go to the Italian deli on Alpine, buy an eggplant sub and a liter of Pellegrino, and walk home. I eat my sandwich, lie on my lawn, mess around with my phone. I google "Mark Mills."

Up pops his website, along with a few tangential mentions on music sites and rock blogs. I click MarkMills.com. One page only. Stark blue, looks homemade. Bands he reps. Contact info. I cut and paste his studio information into my cell. Ridiculous. So easy. Who the hell is this guy? How did he get with D. Webb?

August 18. Roughly a month before she went missing. I scroll through Gmail trying to sort out where I was the day she was posing for those pictures. A few nonsense emails from Lee ("Blow me." And, "Come over. Come sit on my face."). A forward from my mother. A Zappos receipt. Nothing noteworthy. I try text next—clicking Kate's name, reading backward, to August 18: "Bitch, you late. Hurry up. Want pie." So, supper club. Thursday. School day. Dakota was living, breathing, getting naked with sketch music managers, scribbling dates down on old army jackets.

Back to Contacts. Mark Mills. I tap his name with two fingers. Consider emailing. Stop myself. Toss my phone into the purple bougainvillea. Roll face-first into dry grass.

31.

We used to do this all the time, me and Lee. Screw around for hours. Order Thai takeout or pizza. Do our homework downstairs in front of the TV while his parents were out at some dinner or fund-raiser or fancy premiere.

Now, no more screwing around. And Lee's big, showy shack makes me feel sad, sick, and lonely.

"Pass that, please?" He points.

We're trading dishes. Shrimp lo mein for pork fried rice. Lee takes a sloppy bite of noodle and makes a face. "Tastes weird, right?"

"What?"

"The lo mein." He chews quickly and pats his mouth with a napkin. "Saltier?"

"Tastes fine to me." I suck on my lip and push the plate away.

"You're done?"

"Yeah."

"You barely ate."

"I did, Lee, I ate, like, half a tub of that eggplant."

"That's nothing. That's like eating *air*."

I shrug him off and grab at the orange chicken. "Look," I say, picking up a glossy piece of meat with my middle finger and thumb. "Mmm." I fake enthusiasm, taking a bite and playfully pushing Lee backward. He's not laughing.

"Knox." He drops his chopsticks.

"What?" I lick my thumb clean and flash my fakest grin. "I'm eating, see?"

"You're miserable."

I don't want to have this conversation right now. I want to pack up my crap and go home. "Lee, I'm fine. I'm tired, okay?"

"You're different."

"Lee."

"It's like, you look at me and it's like—" He looks at me. "Like I make you sick or something."

"Stop."

"No, I just—I want to talk about it."

"There's nothing to talk about."

"I just—I can't tell if it's her?" he says, breathing hard. "Or if it's *me*." We watch each other. "Is it me?"

"Is *what* you?"

"You don't, like, let me touch you anymore."

"That's not true."

"It *is*." His eyes are wet. "Why can't you just admit it?"

"Admit *what*? Lee. Jesus, *stop*. You're freaking out over nothing."

"It's not nothing. God, Adrienne. You're showing up drunk to dinners, you're completely withdrawn, you're dressing different—"

"You *like* this," I say, grabbing at my dress, incensed. "You *prefer* it, remember?"

"Prefer it to *what*?"

"You said I looked sexy."

"You do! You did and you do."

"So—what is this?" I scream, not looking at him, looking at the shiny walls instead. "You're pissed off because I won't *fuck* you?!"

"Oh my god, Adrienne." His voice cracks and one arm flies up, accidentally knocking the takeout container out of my hand. Orange chicken skitters across the Turkish rug.

"I'm sorry," he whispers quickly, looking humiliated and apologetic. I dart toward the blinking television, where the white rectangular box lies, mangled, nearby on its side. "It's fine," I say, digging bits of fried batter out of the carpet.

"I didn't mean to—"

"It's okay, Lee." I right myself, carrying the mess to the trash can. "I wasn't hungry anyway."

32.

Open period. Julian and I share a cigarette inside his Datsun.

"This thing work?" I ask, straining to roll down the sealed side window.

"Jammed," he says, biting the cigarette, touching his tongue to its filter. "You need to, like—" He stretches across the seat, using both hands to joggle the window roller. "There." He pulls back, both elbows brushing my thighs. "Air."

"Thanks."

"Finish it," he says, passing me the last of the cig.

I squish the wet filter between my fingers. Touch the damp part to my lips. "I googled that guy," I say, dragging lightly, holding the smoke in. "I have his info. I think we should contact him." I exhale, bracing myself for Julian's wrath, but—

"I can't stop thinking about, just, like, the two of them."

"Maybe he'll talk to us . . . ?" I say quietly, seizing my moment. Julian's willing, I feel it. Ready to yield. "Maybe he knows something?"

"Maybe he *did* something," he suggests.

I look over. His face is fuchsia.

"Those freakin' pictures," he says, putting his head in his hands. "And I keep going over those dates. A few overlap with shows, but the bulk of them—there's no pattern. I can't link them to anything specific."

I have nothing to offer. No theories, no fantasy scenarios. I feel bad for him. Jilted beau. Betrayed bandmate. "Want me to do it? I can call him," I say. "Try to set something up?"

He's zoned out, hunched over, chewing a knuckle. After a minute: "Don't do that," he says, snapping back to life. "No, I know the guy." He faces me. "I know where to find him."

33.

The Echo.

Julian knows the door guy. We skate by with quick waves—no IDs, no dollars. Inside, it's black, packed, and L-shaped. There're mirrors. There's a bar. Onstage, three girls beat drums and scream melodiously into mics. Julian leads me up front. We meet the crowd, scanning lit faces.

"What does he look like?"

"Dunno. Old. Shithead vibe."

We squint, searching. I gesture left. "That guy?"

Not that guy.

We wait. Check our watches, watch the door, watch the show. We buy drinks. Between sets, we buy more drinks. New band: loud, goth, grating. I'm ready to go.

"Can we leave?" I scream, having hit my death-metal limit.

Julian shrugs.

"He's not here," I say.

"Okay."

"Okay?"

He nods. We head out. Then: *"There."* Julian points. "Right there."

By the bar, a forty-something aging rocker—leather skin, shaggy hair—sips amber liquid from a clear plastic tumbler. "Stay here."

"Wait, why?"

"Because. You're a girl. Guy's a creep."

"So? Why am I here, then? I'm coming."

"No way."

"I am."

"Adrienne."

We glare at each other. "I *am*."

He relents. "Whatever." We weedwack forward.

Mills looks past us, at the stage. His head bops. Julian slaps his shoulder. Mills smiles back, polite-like, grips his arm, then looks away. Julian leans close. Says something I can't hear. Mills pulls back, drags a pack of Camels from his coat, then heads to the back of the club. We follow him out to the patio. He lights his smoke. Then, out of nowhere, Julian pummels the guy.

My heart flies to my throat. People part like the red sea. I scream and yank Julian's jacket, pulling him backward. He's wailing, shouting, "What did you do to her?! She was *eighteen*. What the fuck did you do?!"

Some random short guy helps me hold Julian back. He's thrashing and bucking like a horse. Everyone stares. Mills blots blood on his sleeve. "I didn't *do* anything. Fuck, dude, my nose."

Julian inhales. Tries to slow his breathing. His face is freaking me out. Huge eyes, veiny forehead, purple cheeks. After a few silent seconds, people go back to their cigarettes. Julian, shrill: "We found pictures."

"Who the hell is 'we'?"

"Me," I say, stepping forward.

"And who the hell are you?"

Julian, sounding sad now, defeated: "She wasn't dressed, man."

"Get me a towel," Mills says. "Someone, please." He's pinching his nose.

I riffle through my purse. Pull two tissues loose. "Here."

He takes them. Tilts his head back. "We were working together," he says, crumpling up the Kleenex. "Those pictures—they were her idea. Cover art. For the demo."

"What demo?"

"*Her* demo."

"She wasn't working on one."

"Dude, she was. And it's freaking beautiful."

Julian looks crestfallen. He shakes out his fist. "Why didn't I know that?"

Soft, sympathetic even: "Look, I don't know. She came to me." Then, as if suddenly remembering that the sociopath he's consoling just pounded him like a veal cutlet: "Jesus, man, why'd you have to fuck my face up?"

"I'm sorry."

"Super sorry," I echo.

Mills, clearly conflicted (missing girl, grieving kids): "I can burn you a disc. Of the demo."

"Really?" I screech, sounding insanely overeager. "We'd like that."

"Wait." Julian again. "Did you—" He's halfway out the door, Mills. "Did you sleep with her?" One final, frantic plea for answers.

MM exhales dramatically. "Dude, *no*. Come on." The tissue I gave him is completely soaked through. "We done?" He's itchy and irritated. "I gotta go deal with my nose."

"August eighteenth," Julian blurts.

"What?"

"The date. On the pictures. August eighteenth."

Mills, perplexed, says, "The processing date?"

Julian raises one hand in surrender. "I'm really sorry, man. About your face."

Mills spits out an aggravated grumble. Saunters off. *Saunters*. Really, truly.

Julian touches my hip. "I messed up."

"You beat the crap out of that guy."

"We should leave," he says. He sounds tired. I am too. "Come on." He pushes me forward, his hand on my hip still. "Walk fast, let's go."

34.

"What is wrong with that woman?"

Five p.m. I'm in the kitchen fixing spiked tea and cookies for Kate. My neighbor is throwing a full-blown fit. "Her boyfriend," I say, dumping scalding water from the kettle into a teapot. "He won't commit."

High-pitched girl-shrieks rattle the ceiling and walls. Kate winces and blocks her ears with balled-up napkins. "She does this a lot?"

I nod.

"She really should move on, don't you think?"

"They've been together awhile." Some dull thudding. "She loves him, I guess?"

Crash.

We both duck. Kate mashes her finger into an oatmeal cookie crumb and continues: "That don't sound like love to me. . . ."

I shrug. Spill some tea into Kate's cup. "Love . . . hate . . ."

"Seriously?"

"Two sides, same coin, don't'cha think?"

She pours two shots' worth of bourbon into her Sleepy-time. Glares at me over her cup rim.

"What?" I laugh. "What's with the look?"

She frowns and lowers her cup. "He's miserable. You know that, right?"

My smile wilts. My insides tense up. The neighbor lets out a shrill string of obscenities. "Who? Crazy Girl's boyfriend?" I ask, feigning oblivion.

Kate's face stays stony. "You're fucking everything up, Knox. Lee loves you and you treat him like shit."

I put my palm flat against the side of the scalding kettle. "It's not the same with me and Lee."

"Right." She sniffs. "Because you spend all your time chasing down a dead girl. Lee's alive. I'm alive. We're right here. And you, you're over there, looking like some goth geek and going on dates with Julian Boyd."

Heat's too much. I yank my hand back—

"You didn't think I knew about that, right?"

—and hide behind my hair. "We're not going on dates," I say.

Kate grabs at two fingers and twists my palm toward the ceiling. "Don't do that to yourself," she scolds, blowing lightly on my burn. Then, "Watch yourself, Adrienne."

I look up.

"I love you," she says, dipping a finger in her cup and sucking off the tea-and-liquor concoction, "but you keep going the way you're going, and you're gonna fall into a big pile of shit."

35.

Eight fifteen a.m. I'm a cartoon burglar tiptoeing down the hall to lit—holding my breath, then peering through the tiny rectangular window to Murphy's classroom. There he is, at the pulpit. And there's Julian in the pews. I back away, chewing my cheeks. I'm sans essay and not facing Murphy until I finish the thing.

I go outside to wait. For what? I twiddle my thumbs and chew a cherry cough drop. I twirl in place. I do it again. Chaîné turns. Pirouettes. I'm twirling and twirling when I smack into something tall, skinny, and warm.

"Crap."

There're two of us on the cement sidewalk, an explosion of papers and books.

"Wyatt."

"*Jesus*, Knox." He's rubbing his shoulder with one hand

and sweeping his stuff into a pile with the other. "Fancy dance moves."

"Sorry, god, sorry." I'm up on my knees and grabbing at smashed loose-leaf.

"My fault," he says. "Wasn't watching the road." He's pretty, up close. Bright but not blinding.

"Here, I'll get this." I lunge for the last of it. Two stiff sheets of notepaper with—*holyshitamazing*—Kate's curly writing.

"That's mine," he says, snatching it back.

"Yours, huh?"

He's all shades of red and scrambling to his feet.

"Sorry about—" He waves at me, still on the ground. "Can you get up?"

"I'm fine," I insist, dazed.

"Great. Good." He's batting the letter. "Bye, then."

"Sure," I say, waving as he walks. "See ya around."

Lunch. Lee's birthday.

Me, Kate, Lee, sharing a sleeve of Fig Newtons and throwing shit (pen caps, paper clips, baby carrots) at each other's faces. We're laughing. I'm in Lee's lap. I'm making an effort. I can be good. I can be a nice girlfriend and a better best friend.

"Missed." Kate's crouching down, smiling. She eats the carrot I tried to nail her nose with.

"Sit up." I take aim again, throw, and—bull's-eye—hit her forehead hard with a pen cap.

"Ow."

Lee and I high-five. I feel good for a sec—bright, cheery—then I don't. Just like that—a momentary flash of something sweet, followed by a whole bunch of nothingness. He squeezes my thigh. "Nice shot."

I smile. Back to faking it.

"Tonight," he says.

"Right, tonight." B-day dinner with Lee's folks. I'm dreading it. I adore them. They'll see straight through me.

"Pick you up at seven?"

I nod.

"Great." Then, "Get up," he instructs. I do. "Getting a Coke. Anyone want anything?"

No one wants anything.

"What?" Kate says after Lee leaves—because I'm grimacing, maybe? Or glaring?

"Write any love sonnets lately?"

"Sorry?"

"Or send any sexy letters?"

Her cheeks flush. She straightens up. "Sonnets? No."

"Katie."

"What?" She's embarrassed. A rarity. The girl barely ever has a vulnerable moment. "I wrote him a note." She shrugs.

"Saying what?"

"'Hi. Stellar weather. Cute boots.'" She pauses. "How do you even know about that?"

"Bumped into him. This morning. Literally, we, like, collided. It fell out of his bag."

"Oh." She sits back. "Well, why hasn't he responded?"

"I don't know."

"Well, why doesn't he love me?"

"Katie." I open my arms and she curls against my chest.

"I'm not pretty enough."

"You're a knockout."

"I'm not slutty enough."

"You're the sluttiest."

I hug her harder. Lee's in the distance with a soda can. He looks so upbeat and moony. I let my gaze float left. There's Murphy. *There's Murphy, crap*, clutching a lunch tray and staring me down.

"Fuck." I let Kate go and sit up.

"What's wrong with you? Why'd the hugging stop?"

"Because. I haven't been to lit since last week and I'm in huge fucking trouble."

She twists around. Spots him. "Oh, right."

I'm not even sure what to do or where to look. For a moment, we just watch each other. Like lovers, only not. Then the head shaking starts. Back and forth and he's wearing

133

this stupid, shitty smile that reads, *Adrienne Knox, you are a WILD disappointment.*

I armor up, preparing for the worst. *Flunk me, suspend me,* whatever it is, I'll eat it.

Then, "Where's he going?" Kate asks.

He's walking away. No confrontation. No lecture.

"I thought for sure you were about to get royally fucked."

Lee's back. "By me? Yes, please."

Kate laughs, but I can't. *Nothing* from Murphy? Not a friendly slap on the wrist or a see-me-after-school?

"You okay?" Lee says, leaning into me.

This feels worse than getting reprimanded, but, "I'm fine," I say with a jovial shrug. "Guess I'm a lost cause."

New resolution: less Julian, more Lee.

Two fifty. On my own at the curb, waiting for Kate to pull the car around. I stare past the median strip to the freak section. There're piles and piles of kids wearing all shades of black, so it takes me a minute to locate him—pale, scruffy, skinny, pretty—squatting in the sun with his smoke. He lifts a hand, shielding his eyes. Then he tips an imaginary hat my way. I wave limply. I feel a tug in my gut. I'm panicking suddenly, *desperate* for Lee. I twist on my heel, scanning the side entrance to the gym, but all I see are frosh Dakota wannabes, dozens of them, with their purple lips and lace. They look like me. I want to flatten them all like potato pancakes. I look back, to Julian, but he's already gone. Kate's car materializes: windows down, heat blasting, Stevie Nicks blaring from the stereo. "Get in," she hollers.

I step off the curb.

36.

Kate and I go to that nauseatingly hip little stretch of Sunset in Silver Lake, where we spend a good hour and a half *not*-buying Lee's birthday gift. By now we've seen inside every book/record/vintage shop on the block. Nothing feels very Lee.

"Dude, time to buy something."

"Right, no, I know."

We're standing inside a comic book store. "I mean, he likes this stuff, he does," I insist, fondling a skinny booklet with a boobalicious cartoon girl on the cover.

"I've never seen him with a comic."

"He has this, like, graphic novel he really likes . . . by this guy . . . shit, what's it called?"

"Why not buy him, like, a baseball bat. At that sports memorabilia place?"

"Because." I blink. "He plays soccer. Not baseball."

"So?" A beat. "Anyways," she rambles on, "it's just a dumb boy-gift. How hard can it be?"

"*Hard*. And you've known the guy pretty much your whole life, so why aren't you more helpful?" I tug her dress playfully, yanking her toward the cashier. Then, "Hi," to the sales dude at the register. Black glasses, tight tee. "You guys do gift cards?"

37.

Musso and Frank.

White tablecloths, surly waiters, dry martinis, chicken potpie.

"Adrienne, honey, you want?" Leslie, Lee's mom, is pushing a plate of french fries forward. She, me, Lee, and Lee's dad, Josh—are all squished into a back booth by the bar.

I take some. "Thanks."

"Sure."

Last year, Leslie had an affair with her Pilates instructor. "Oh, here, honey. Ketchup."

"Thank you."

Josh went ape-shit. Lee had a mini-meltdown. Everyone went to therapy. They're better now. Pretty much.

"The remodel looks great," I blather, feeling a fast pang of shame. "I got a quick peek last week when I was at the house." Newly redone bedroom and master bath.

"Great, right?" Josh now. "Terrific contractor."

I nod. And, "Here," I say to Lee, sliding his gift card sideways.

"Already? You're sure?"

"Yeah." I'm eager to get the gift giving over with.

"Thanks." We kiss quickly. Lee drops his fork and slides a finger under the envelope flap. "Oh." His chin wrinkles. "Oh, cool. Knox, thank you."

"You have that one graphic novel you like . . . ?"

"*Blankets*. Craig Thompson."

"Right. I thought I'd get you something similar, but then I couldn't remember the name of the book. Figured I'd let you choose something new." I smile insanely. Josh and Leslie smile back. Lee's smiling too. "Is it okay?" I say, feeling pathetically low.

"Hey, I love it." He puts his hand in my hair. Leans into me. Nudges me sweetly with the top of his head.

38.

Tuesday. Six fourteen a.m. I'm in bed still, hitting snooze, trying to prolong a happy dream: Kate and me eating custardy flan on a San Francisco trolley. My cell bleeps. I bolt upright, eyes closed still, and feel around for it.

"Hello?" My voice comes out raspy and broken.

"It's Julian."

I rub my face to wake up. "Everything okay?"

"Yeah."

"It's early."

"Couldn't sleep."

"Do you even *have* my number? How are you calling me?"

"Magic."

Happy rush. I swing my legs over the edge of the bed. "So. Hi, I guess?"

"Hi." He sucks in some smoke. "I'm outside."

"Outside, where?"

"Like, outside, on your doorstep. Which one's your room?"

Instant sweat. I run to my window. There's Julian, on the lawn, looking left at my neighbor's apartment. "What're you doing here?"

"Proposition. Which one's yours? The one with the curtains?"

"Just—stay there, okay? And keep quiet, please? People are sleeping." *I hope.* I toss my phone to the floor, pull a pair of jeans off my desk chair, and throw a hoodie over my nightgown. Real quick, I scrub my teeth. Then I slip out the front door as quietly as I can. It's freezing out. I tuck my hands under my armpits.

"So?" I say, but all I can think about is my bare face and ratty hair. Julian looks like Julian. Beaten beauty. No fair.

"Feel like taking a trip?"

"We have class in an hour and a half."

"So?"

"So?"

He smiles.

"Come to the beach with me."

"*No.*"

"Come on, you like the beach."

Used to. "How would you know?" I jog in place. "It's freezing." And, "Anyways, I can't. I can't go anywhere with you."

"Why not?"

Lee. "Because."

He looks at me, really *looks* at me, and I feel my will weaken.

"You're considering it. I see the wheels turning."

How much more damage can I possibly do?

I shove the door open. "Go wait in the car, okay? Just—give me twenty minutes to shower and change."

We take the 101 south to the 110 south to the 10 west. We empty out onto Ocean Avenue. Park at the pier. Big surprise. Julian and I continue our tour of depressing Dakota landmarks. Today's stop: Suicide City.

"You okay?" he asks. "You comfortable?"

We're in sweaters and jackets in a pocket of dirty beach. To our left, tacked to the pier deck, an overblown, rainbow memorial dedicated to C. Chang and D. Webb. Photos, flowers, streamers, ribbons—we stay away.

"I'm okay," I say, feeling a pretty even mix of good and bad. Dakota death site? *Bad.* Julian Boyd? *Good*, sometimes. Like now.

We watch the water. We watch the park on the pier: Ferris wheel. Crap food stands. Carousel. I go, "Goldfish the goldfish."

"Sorry?"

"Goldfish the goldfish," I say. "Clever name, right? He was a gift, from Dakota. We were eleven."

"Nice gift."

I shake some sand off my hands. "He lived a year and a half."

"That's, like, forever in fish years."

"Right?"

Julian leans all the way back, flat to the ground. "She was a shitty girlfriend," he says. "She dicked around a lot."

"Other guys?" I ask cautiously. Even though I know this. Or knew it. Rumors.

"Other guys," he echoes, dusting his hands against the sides of his thighs.

"So why'd you stay with her?"

He rolls over. "She was—" His eyebrows bounce up. "I don't know, ya know?" Shrugs. "We were like magnets."

I wince, having a flash: Dakota and Julian on the quad, kissing. Me watching from Kate's car after school. Dakota in his lap, two sexy misfits sharing the sexiest smoke.

"You think I'm weak?" he asks.

I get down on the ground with him, so we're level. "That's not what I think." I think about me and Lee. How pedestrian our love is. How frumpy and unromantic. "She was a shitty friend," I offer. He blinks, earnestly, gratefully. My heart shakes. "Not your fault, you know?" I'm shitty. I'm the shittiest. I'm the worst girlfriend. I'm *her*.

"Hold this?" Julian passes me his lighter and cigarette pack. Then he reaches into his back pocket and pulls free a tiny Baggie. Floorboard drugs. "You want?" He waves around the plastic. Inside: four dead, curly mushrooms.

I sit up. "You're not serious." He's already eating two.

"Have 'em." He shakes the bag under my nose. "They taste great."

I take the bag. Pull one out. It's dusty and stiff. I sniff at it. "I've never . . ." Am I really doing this? Is this who I am now? The girl who skips school to eat mushrooms with the boy who isn't her boyfriend?

"Live a little," Julian says.

So I eat one. It tastes hideous. Rotten and woodsy and, "You're right. Just like candy." I quickly swallow the last of it: one long, skinny stem. Then, "What happens now?"

"I dunno. We wait, I guess."

"I'm scared." I'm laughing, but I'm petrified.

"Don't be," he says, and takes my hand.

Later.

Everything is slow and humming. Julian's hand feels spongy. I keep crushing his fingers over and over again, slipping backward into the sand and squashing him hard because he tells me he likes it when I grip really tight.

"You okay?" Julian asks.

I roll over. I feel so clean. I walk to the water and say a prayer for dead Cassidy Chang. My cheeks are wet, why are my cheeks wet? Julian says, "You're crying."

"I thought you were back over there." I point.

"I'm right here."

"Hi."

"Why so sad?"

"I'm not."

"You are, look." He wipes my face with his fingertips. "See?" His hand's all wet.

"I don't *feel* sad," I say.

"Are you sure?"

I'm not. The waves are too loud—crashing, whooshing—I can barely hear myself think. Then, "I *am* sad," I say, suddenly. "I am so sad."

"Told you." He touches my upper arm. "Hey, say my name."

"Julian."

"Say it again."

"Julian."

"Does that sound weird to you?"

It doesn't, so, "No." My chest feels buzzy and bright. "Wanna go for a swim?"

He shakes his head and walks back to the beach. I kick off my shoes and tuck my dress into the waistband of my tights. I wade in. It's icy and right. I go deeper, up to my thighs. I look down at my dress. *Dakota wears black*. I whirl around. Julian's watching me. "Who do I look like?" I ask, calling back to the beach.

Julian says, "You know."

"I don't," I say.

"Come'ere, let's talk."

I trudge back through the water and sand. I sit down. Julian takes off his jacket and wraps it around my damp legs. "Who do I look like?" I ask again.

"You look like you."

"You're sure?"

"You're dressed like someone else."

"Who's that?"

"Can't say her name."

"Why not?"

"Come'ere, come closer." He puts an arm out. "Let's lie down."

I fold up against his cool chest. He wraps his arm around my shoulder.

All over now.

Ten to six and dark out. Julian's parked a block away from my house, engine off. "You okay?" he asks.

I feel stupid and spent, but, "Fine," I say, not looking up.

He screws with his key chain. "You sorry we did that?" Tears, drugs—intimacy minus the sex.

"No." I shrug, collecting all my crap from the glove compartment: wallet, keys, cell. Two missed calls from Mom. Five from Lee.

"Trouble?"

"Yup."

He bats the stick shift with his fist. I pop the lock and push on the door with one knee. "Thanks for the drugs."

Julian smiles. He says, "You sure you're okay?"

I tug the sun visor down and check my reflection. I look hellish—my mascara streaked and smudged. "I am," I tell him. And maybe I'm lying and maybe I'm not. "Anyways, I wanted to come."

39.

I'm buying my own cigarettes now.

"Can I bum one?"

The ones Dakota smoked, with the white, hollow filters. "Here." I pass my pack to the freshman with the blue button-down and sloppy bun.

"Thanks."

My free period. I'm chain-smoking. There's Julian, across the quad, *staring*. We're locked in some crazy glare-off— thirty psycho seconds—and I know it's the dress, not me. It's Dakota's. I put it on this morning because I felt shitty and dumb and remarkably low. So he's staring and staring, but then he turns around and walks away as if stolen dresses and missing girls just don't matter at all.

At lunch, Kate gets me drunk on gin. About the dress she says, "Who died?" I don't reply. The answer seems blindingly obvious.

"Where were you yesterday?"

"Home sick," I say.

"Sure you were."

"Where's Lee?"

"There." She points sideways, not looking up. Lee's sitting on a rock by the auditorium with Alice. They're sharing one of those big cafeteria cookies and laughing like their lives are just so fucking hilarious.

"He called you nine billion times yesterday."

"So?"

"So, you didn't call him back." She doesn't sound angry, or particularly impassioned. She sounds over it. "What do you expect?"

I eat some of Kate's candy bar, picking pieces of brittle chocolate off the tin wrapper. I think about losing Lee. I can't tell if I care. I feel exhaustingly blank, as if someone wiggled up inside me and sucked out my soul with a vacuum cleaner.

I go see Griffin in Guidance. Because Murphy suggested it. Because my head might implode.

"I'm going crazy," I tell her.

We're in an air-conditioned room with no windows. Griffin's wearing a silk tank and thin cardigan. She looks reasonable. Levelheaded. She says, "Crazy, how?"

"Like, I dunno, like, *crazy*. Like, my thoughts won't stop."

She uncrosses then recrosses her legs.

"They're not good thoughts, though, you know?" I say. "My boyfriend's mom, she, like, dicked around a lot last year. Like, had an affair? I think I'm like that. I think I'm fickle." My eyes well up.

Griffin grabs a tissue box off her desk. Hands it to me. "Okay." A beat. "Okay, you know, though, you can be whoever you want to be. You realize that, right? You're in control, Adrienne." She grins reassuringly. "*You* choose your path."

"This doesn't—" I wave both hands around, frustrated, super confused. "This doesn't feel like a choice," I say. "I'm not *me* anymore. I don't know where I went."

After school, I walk to my bus thinking of all the things I once hated that now I genuinely love. Gold jewelry. Rod Stewart. Tuna fish sandwiches. And Lee? I loved him last month and last year, but now? What's real? I wish I could tell, but I can't anymore.

". . . they found a boot."

Someone says this. Who? I whip around and find two slight freshman girls in hats and bangles, gnawing their hair.

"A boot?"

"Yeah, black. The dad identified it."

"Where?"

"Beach. Low tide."

My heart goes berserk. "Whose boot?" I demand, interjecting as if it's my business.

Both turn, blinking. One shrugs, says, "I don't—"

"Whose dad?" I ask, not letting her finish.

"Dakota Webb's."

Everything inside sinks. "How do you know that?"

"My brother," says the one wearing the floppy felt hat. "He's LAPD."

My vision blurs. My neck is on fire. I have to brace myself against the bus to keep myself from falling.

"Was she your friend?" asks the one with the bracelets and overbite. "Dakota," she says, squinting. "Were you two close?"

I tune them out, turning away. A hand creeps up my arm. "Hi," Julian says. He smells like cigarettes and soap.

"They found a boot," I blurt. "A girl's boot on the beach."

"I know."

"You *know*?"

His mouth is tight. "Talk of the town," he says glumly.

We watch each other. "This means something, right?" More staring. Julian looks so regular. Regular face, regular day.

"Come on," he says, pulling me forward. "I'm taking you home."

Sam's out, so we go to my room. We lie on my silky bedspread. On my nightstand is half a glass of water, *Jane Eyre*, and my blue plastic retainer case. Julian fingers the fringe around the neck of Dakota's dress.

"It's not mine," I say, even though I know he knows it's not.

"Looks nice on you, though." His hand is on my neck. His hand is in my hair. For the first time in forever I actually feel something. It's fuzzy and kinetic and it takes me a second to identify. He tugs my ponytail, lightly, like he's kidding, and that's when it hits me.

"Adrienne?"

This is noisy, dizzying lust.

We're kissing. He's on top of me. His hands are on my face and he's shaking. I'm shaking. He tastes like Chap Stick and cigarettes and something sour. I like it. I kiss harder, tug his shirt off, wrap my thighs around my hips. This feels like a fit. Like, *right*. Like a massive, monumental relief. I want to stay this way—Julian smashed into me, his torso locked between my legs—forever. Dakota's dress is shoved up around my chest and my underwear is in a ball by my feet. I undo Julian's pants, push his boxers down. My head is off the bed so he grabs it with two hands and makes me look at him—his eyes glassy and wide, and I know what he's thinking because I'm thinking the same thing myself: *Who the hell are you, Adrienne Knox?*

"Stop," I say.

"Stop?"

"Yeah, stop, please." I roll out from under him, pulling Dakota's dress down. "I can't," I say. But I can, *I could*.

Julian yanks his boxers up. He's splotchy and breathless and there're claw marks on one shoulder. "I'm sorry, I thought . . ."

"I know."

"Adrienne?"

I'm still crazy on fire. Julian touches my hand and I *can't*— I recoil. "If I hadn't been wearing the dress?"

"Hey . . ."

"This isn't me, you see that, right? I'm not like this."

"Like what?"

"Like, *careless*. Like, *this*. Like . . . like . . ." Like *her*. "Please go," I say.

"Why?" He pulls his jeans back on over his boxers. "We don't have to do anything else. I can stay."

"You have to go," I tell him. And I don't turn around or say I'm sorry or say good-bye. "Please?"

He gets up.

40.

Later: I'm freshly showered, tightly wound, ready for bed. I'm making figure eights with bare feet on fuzzy carpet—two steps left, two right, a quick pivot. An easy sequence, so I keep at it. My legs are Jell-O. My mind snowy. No more Julian. No more beached boots. Just me, my moves, and the blue binder resting against the leg of my desk.

Blue binder.

Its corners are peeling. Papers poke out the sides like an overloaded cheese sandwich. Why didn't I see it sooner? Did he leave it here on purpose? No, right? I made him go too fast. Barely dressed. Hard, still. The binder got left behind.

I bring it to the bed. Peek inside. *Jane* notes. *Frankennotes*. It's Julian's lit binder. I leaf through, quickly, greedily, searching for something, but what? His heart? Soul? I want him back, suddenly. I want him *on* me, on top, *crushing* me. I slam the binder shut and sit for a sec, then open it back up.

Graded *Jane* essay. A–. *How?* Dude's girlfriend goes missing and he still manages to keep up with school assignments?

I flip further. A bunch of blank loose-leaf. Four sheets of eyeball doodles. Then, last few pages, I see this:

i'm sorry i'm sorry i'm sorry i'm sorry dakota
so sorry so sorry so sorry dakota i'm sorry i'm
sorry i'm sorry i'm sorry dakota so sorry so sorry
so sorry dakota i'm sorry i'm sorry i'm sorry i'm
sorry dakota so sorry so sorry so sorry dakota
i'm sorry i'm sorry i'm sorry i'm sorry dakota
so sorry so sorry so sorry dakota i'm sorry i'm
sorry i'm sorry i'm sorry dakota so sorry so sorry
so sorry dakota i'm sorry i'm sorry i'm sorry i'm
sorry dakota so sorry so sorry so sorry dakota
i'm sorry i'm sorry i'm sorry i'm sorry dakota so
sorry so sorry so sorry dakota i'm sorry i'm sorry
i'm sorry i'm sorry dakota so sorry so sorry so
sorry dakota i'm sorry i'm sorry i'm sorry i'm
sorry dakota so sorry so sorry so sorry dakota
i'm sorry i'm sorry i'm sorry i'm sorry dakota so
sorry so sorry so sorry dakota i'm sorry i'm sorry
i'm sorry i'm sorry dakota so sorry so sorry so
sorry dakota i'm sorry i'm sorry i'm sorry i'm
sorry dakota so sorry so sorry so sorry dakota
i'm sorry i'm sorry i'm sorry i'm sorry dakota

so sorry so sorry so sorry dakota i'm sorry i'm
sorry i'm sorry i'm sorry dakota so sorry so sorry
so sorry dakota i'm sorry i'm sorry i'm sorry i'm
sorry dakota so sorry so sorry so sorry dakota
i'm sorry i'm sorry i'm sorry i'm sorry dakota
so sorry so sorry so sorry dakota i'm sorry i'm
sorry i'm sorry i'm sorry dakota so sorry so sorry
so sorry dakota i'm sorry i'm sorry i'm sorry i'm
sorry dakota so sorry so sorry so sorry dakota
i'm sorry i'm sorry i'm sorry i'm sorry dakota
so sorry so sorry so sorry dakota i'm sorry i'm
sorry i'm sorry i'm sorry dakota so sorry so sorry
so sorry dakota i'm sorry i'm sorry i'm sorry i'm
sorry dakota so sorry so sorry so sorry dakota
i'm sorry i'm sorry i'm sorry i'm sorry dakota so
sorry so sorry so sorry dakota i'm sorry i'm sorry
i'm sorry i'm sorry dakota so sorry so sorry so
sorry dakota i'm sorry i'm sorry i'm sorry i'm
sorry dakota so sorry so sorry so sorry dakota

No punctuation or capitalization, just one long run-on; a
marathon apology. It goes on forever. It's fucking crazy. I hop
off the bed and slam the binder shut, as if what's inside might
bite or beat me if I let it.

41.

I'm on Dakota's lawn, watching her bedroom window. Emmett's home. His Ford sedan is parked next to Dakota's Jeep. I'm skipping phys ed, lab, and lit. I'm here to snoop. I need answers. But Emmett? Why's he home?

My cell bleeps. Text from Julian: *Midway thru Murphy. Where you at?* I picture the boy in my bed. I feel a flicker of arousal, then guilt-out about it. More circular thinking: *Why so sorry? What's he done?* I look left at Emmett's car. Okay. I'm leaving. Then:

"Who's here?"

The front door creaks open. Emmett, dressed in green-and-gray fleece, is clutching a newspaper with one hand and shading his eyes from the sun with the other. "Adrienne? Is that you?"

Crap.

"It's me," I say, real meek, suddenly nauseated. Emmett

in the flesh. "I'm sorry," I say, crossing the lawn. "I should've called, come sooner. I meant to stop by."

"That's okay, honey, come'ere, let me see you."

I walk a ways till we're standing face-to-face. "Not much to see." I shrug. It's been years. He looks older. Less hair, more lines. Sad too. But he always looked sad.

"You're all grown."

"I guess."

He stares. His eyes water and I have to look away.

Inside, I sit at the dining room table clutching a hot mug of milky tea. Emmett stands, gulping coffee. He steps sideways, away from the window, and a claw-shaped shadow falls onto his face. For a split second he's 200 percent terrifying. Eyes like pits. Switchblades for cheekbones. I see it: early morning, dead Dakota being dragged by her hair to the garage. Emmett shoving her into the Jeep. Driving them both to the beach. Tossing her off the pier.

I shiver. The light shifts. Emmett smiles and the black fantasy fades. Now he's docile. Sweet and broken. "Your mom called," he says. "We talked for a bit. That was nice."

"Oh, I know," I say brightly, overcompensating. "She mentioned." I glance at the steps. Feel bad about the break-in. Stolen dress. Swiped pictures.

He follows my gaze. "Go upstairs," he offers. "Take what you like."

A small sound escapes my lips.

"It's okay, I want you to. All of it—her stuff—it's just sitting there. Not being used."

I feel absolutely transparent. I scooch back and forth uneasily in my chair.

Bedroom. I'm here and it's legal. I don't waste too much time thinking about how weird this is—me up here, Emmett downstairs. I start searching. Anything that might incriminate Julian. First, one overall sweep: her drawers, behind the bureau, under the bed, the hamper. What do I expect? More drugs? Julian would never intentionally hurt anyone, would he? Could he have bought bad pills? Could she have overdosed? Maybe he panicked? Tried to make it look like a suicide? Could you do that to someone you love? *Do away with them?* Dump them in a pond, a ditch, the big, scary sea?

I feel funny. My head, a helium balloon.

I recheck her closet, riffle through the CD bins, press each floorboard—searching for new secret spots. Nothing. I sit for a bit.

Bookshelves: old textbooks; novels for lit (*Huck Finn, Lolita, A Raisin in the Sun*); a year's worth of *Rolling Stone* issues, stacked; one Langley yearbook. I touch the spine. Slide it forward. Flip through to Dakota's freshman portrait. Page 172. There she is: black-and-white. Square and small.

She looks her age. Fourteen. I haven't seen this thing in years. I stare for a while. She's the real deal. My friend. The girl she was *before* high school hit. Before rock music, sex, and a yen for popularity flattened her sweet streak.

Slipping the book back on the shelf, I see it. A photo corner jutting out the top. I pinch it. Pull slowly. My belly bottoms out.

Me. It's *me*. I'm twelve, maybe? Thirteen? I'm licking an ice cream cone. My eyes are crossed. Did she take this?

Proof, finally. Of our friendship. I mattered once.

Even if I don't anymore.

42.

Six p.m. and dark already. Sam and Mom are downstairs clinking pots, NPR on full blast. My room smells like fried potatoes.

Ding.

How much longer till I'm sane again? Is the not knowing what makes this particular brand of bad so miserable? If I knew Dakota was, for sure, dead, would I feel any better? Do I need all the gritty particulars to move on? The whodunits? The whys?

The photo I took earlier is stuck to the corkboard above my mirror. I stare at it. I look happy.

Ding.

I grab my crying cell. New text.

Outside, it says. *Know you're home. Left my lit binder. Bring out front?*

Julian, of course. My heart palpitates. No happiness here.

I grab the binder off my bed, ripping the *i'm sorry* stuff from the back and shoving it into my book bag. Safer to have.

Now, standing two or three feet away from him, my body is turned toward his car. I can't completely face him. "Here," I say, handing him the binder, my fingers quaking like I've just eaten a whole pile of Ritalin.

"Thanks."

I stand there. Afraid to move. Certain a premature exit might seem super conspicuous.

"I'm sorry," he blurts. "About yesterday. I shouldn't have—I have these feelings and I shouldn't have—"

"Stop it," I say. "Just *stop*, okay?" Why is he trying to make things right with me? With *me*? It's not me he has to make things right with.

"I like you, Adrienne. I feel connected to you."

"Please stop?" I plead. "I have Lee." *Confess*, I think, willing it telepathically.

Crickets.

"Is there something you want to say?" I ask.

"I'm trying."

"No." Not the sex stuff. *Forget* the sex stuff. "Is there something you need to, like, get off your chest? Like, is there something you need to tell me?"

"I told you, I—" A small shriek leaks from his lips. We

stare at each other. "What do you want me to say?" he asks. "Tell me, please. I'll say it."

"I don't . . ."

He looks so eager and earnest. As if he has no clue what I'm getting at.

"You really don't . . . ?" Is he messing with me? Was I wrong? Did I misread the fine print? Was all that binder bullshit just meaningless dribble?

"Adrienne, hey." He reaches out.

"Adrienne?" My name again. Only this time it's Sam. "You wanna eat or no?"

"One sec," I shout back. Then, to Julian: "I should . . ."

"Right."

"See you at school?"

He shakes his head, back and forth, like, *no no no*, only, "Sure" is what he says instead. "See you tomorrow, I guess."

43.

No more new me.

I'm at school early, scrubbed clean and wearing my old clothes: blue tee, Levi's, huaraches, Sam's wooly cardigan. I'm camped out in front of Lee's locker, clutching my *Jane* essay and dancing around like an overenergized twit. Essay finished, finally, and *fuck*, it's bad, but I stayed up all night reading, writing, rewriting, so now I'm wired and spent—all caffeinated, guilty, and hot.

"Primary colors. For a change." Kate's here. Taunting and tugging my damp hair. "No more raccoon eyes?" Squinting and inspecting me. "Jesus, Knox." Her smile fades. "You okay?"

No. Or, I dunno, *maybe.* "Why?"

"You look like shit. You sleep?"

I shake my head. Four a.m.: I deleted Dakota's voicemail and dumped her dress in the outdoor trash.

"Shower?"

"Yes, fuck you." I grab at my hair. "This is water, not grease."

I get it now. *Really, truly.* Dakota Webb? Not coming back. Gone four weeks. There's no magic mystery to unravel and *fuck* bullshit clues. She's dead and she's wrecking my life.

"You just—you look . . ."

"I know what I look like."

Kate drops her bag on the ground, then starts rummaging through the front compartment. "Here." She passes me her makeup tote. "Put on some lipstick."

I pick out a pink tube of gloss and mindlessly rub a smear of it over my dry lips. "Lee here yet?" I need him. Am ready to repent, beg, make amends.

"Don't know."

I'll be who he needs—I swear it, pledge it, promise.

"Gimme that."

I pass the gloss back. I'm so guilty and sorry I can't see straight. My eyes go all bad and blurry, and before I can blink back tears, I'm bawling.

"Hey, Knox . . ."

"I'm sorry."

"Knox, hey, come 'ere." Kate's hand is on my head. We're hugging. "It's okay . . ."

"It's not."

"It *is*, it's okay." She pulls back.

"I'm sorry."

"What for?"

"I'm just—I'm ready for things to go back to how they were. I can be myself again. I can get better grades and be a better friend and I can make stuff right. With Lee."

"Oh, Knox . . ." Her face changes—it's a subtle shift, but I see it.

"What? What's wrong?"

"No, it's just—" She looks sideways, quickly. "Have you talked to him?"

"Why?"

"You should talk to Lee, Knox."

Cue Lee, stage left, coming through the side door with no-boobs Alice Reed. They're backlit. It's a movie moment. Plot point two for Lee Dixon—where he dumps his crazy-whore girlfriend and takes up with the sunshiney schoolgirl who's been eyeing him since tenth grade.

"So, what, they're, like, legit?" I ask Kate, the pit in my gut expanding.

"I don't know."

Lee passes by, doesn't stop, won't look over.

"It's fine," I say, righting myself, pulling my bag strap over my head. "I know it's my fault," I say, and smile while wiping my wet cheeks.

• • •

I spend lunch alone in an empty bio lab, eating a sleeve of saltines. White, salty cardboard—the least challenging thing I can think to eat.

Dingaling.

My fucking PHONE. That thing only rings with bad business. I grab for it. "Hello?" I sound overeager and shrill.

Nothing. No *hi* back. Just that *stupid*, old-hat silence. I check the ID screen—blocked, of course. "Who *is* this?"

There's actual breathing this time. My head goes berserk. My heart does something speedy and rough. It's *her.* I know it's her. "Dakota?" I whisper, disbelieving, *believing*, fully freaked out.

"I—" There's a girlish sigh on the other end of the line, followed by, "I'm so sorry."

I'm weeping, *instantly.* Hopeful, panicked: "Dakota?" I try again. "I—"

"Adrienne," she says, sounding mousy and wrong. "This isn't—this is Alice. *Reed.*" Oh shit. "I'm sorry, I—" Oh shit, oh *shit.* "I shouldn't have called." The line dies.

44.

Last period, lit. Julian's MIA. I'm zoned out all through
Murphy's lecture, still reeling from Alice's call. Obsessing
over Dakota and Lee and *i'm sorry*s and naked boys.

Then later:

"You."

"Me." It's after class and I'm at Murphy's desk, waving
impishly and tearing through my bag for my *Jane* essay.

"Adrienne . . ." He rubs his head.

"I know, I *know* . . ." *Found it.* I pep up, dropping the
crumpled packet onto his laptop.

"What's this?"

"It's late, it's super late, and I know there's a chance I
won't get credit, just—*please* read it. I worked really hard."

"Adrienne." His brow is arched. "We had a deal."

"We did. I know we did."

"I can't." He passes the paper back. "It's too late."

Stonewalled. I try again: "Please."

"*Adrienne.*" He gets up. "You have to learn."

"I am."

"No, about consequence." He picks up the computer and slides it into his canvas tote. "I gave you two extensions."

"I know you did."

"*Two.*" His face is red and veiny. "I believed in you. I was—I *am*—invested in you succeeding."

"So how is this"—I gesture back and forth between us—"me *succeeding*?" I'm pissed now—ready to repent but getting shut down.

"You can still bring your grade up. It's not too late, okay? You take an incomplete on *Jane Eyre* and you work like crazy the rest of the quarter."

I exhale. My eyes blur. "*Shit.*" I swipe at them—trying to rub away my tears.

"Adrienne . . ." His voice is soft.

"God, *fuck.*" I look at him through glassy eyes. "I fucked it up. Everything is so, so fucked up."

"Adrienne . . ."

"You say my name a lot."

"Come on, come outside, okay?" He throws a hand forward, stepping sideways. His knee cracks. "Come on, walk me out."

Outside it's LA's version of icy weather: low fifties and dull skies. I hold my sweater close to my body and shuffle alongside Murphy. I've stopped crying.

"You sure you're okay?"

I start up again. Ugly blubbering. I miss Lee. Murphy pulls me into a loose embrace and I sob against his jersey polo. He pats my head and I feel momentarily, inexplicably turned on. I jerk back.

"Hey . . ."

"Sorry. Sorry, sorry!" I rub my face, feeling gross and weird and out of my fucking groin, *mind*, whatever.

"What's up with you?"

I shake my head till I'm sick with dizziness. "Don't know. Maybe I'm having some sort of psychological break." I laugh, but mean it. What if I'm crazy? "My boyfriend—we broke up."

"I'm sorry."

"I mean, I *think*. I think we broke up." We walk across the grassy quad, through to the faculty lot. "Did you know . . . ?" I trail off.

"What?" His expression is warm. "Did I know what?" He smells faintly of spicy men's deodorant. I like it. "Did you know Dakota Webb?" I ask quietly. "I mean, did she have you for lit?"

His smile dies. "Last year."

"She was my friend," I say quickly. "A long time ago." He

doesn't reply. He doesn't try to coddle or comfort me. "I hated her," I hear myself say. "For a long time I really hated her. I didn't miss her, or wish nice things for her, I just—I wanted her to feel unloved and miserable." I stop, checking Murphy for signs of horror and shock. But he's facing forward still, stone-faced. "Then she died," I add, and that's when he looks at me. He's white like snow. "She just *died*," I say, *knowing* it, believing it, finally. "Now it's different, you know? I don't hate her anymore."

We've stopped walking. We're facing each other. Murphy pulls a set of keys from his computer bag. "I didn't know you two . . ." He doesn't finish. "I'm really sorry, Adrienne. You must be . . ." He shakes his head. "I'm bad with things like this. Gwen bitches about how hopeless I am with emotional stuff." He smiles past his pastiness.

I point at his shirt. "Sorry," I say. There's a wet spot where I cried.

He tugs on his jersey, looking down. "No sweat." And, "You need a lift somewhere?" He gestures left, to his car.

"Oh, I—"

His car. *His fucking car.* We've been standing three inches from—*holy crap*—from a yellow VW Bug. I'm sick. I've been drop-kicked. "That yours?" I manage.

He walks to the driver's door and undoes the lock. "Gwen's dad's. We keep it in the spare garage. I don't drive it much, but the Honda has a busted carburetor." He runs a hand over the oval roof. "Ugly, right? It's a tin can. Pete—my father-in-law—he's sentimental." He smiles, sheepish. Nevada plates. Massive dent by the back left wheel. *Yellow and dented and old.*

I can't speak or *breathe*, barely—and I must be pale as paper, because Murphy's eyes are forming question marks. "Adrienne, you okay?"

"I . . ." What the fuck. What the hell is happening? *No way* this is some nutty coincidence. What business does he have driving Dakota places? Or *me*, for that matter? "I have to go," I stutter, backing up.

"Adrienne?"

45.

I sprint, *tear*, down a residential street off Melrose—just four blocks to cover between bus stop and ranch home.

Murphy.

Murphy all along.

My high school lit teacher. The guy who grades my papers and threatens me with Griffin in Guidance, the guy with the wife and newborn.

I stop, breathe hard, check the house number with the address I have scrawled on my wrist in black Sharpie. It's a match. I knock. The door swings open. There's Julian, looking boyish. Maybe it's the bare feet, or his mussed hair and Zeppelin T-shirt—but whatever it is, he looks human and sweet.

"Hi, come in," he says, yanking me forward. "Come upstairs," he says, taking my hand.

His place is so *regular*. Fuzzy carpet and taupe walls and the soft murmur of a distant television. We go to his room. It's ferociously neat. Laundry, folded. Bed, made. I wonder if he did a quick clean-job when he got my frantic call.

"Sit."

I sit on the floor. So does he. He looks tight and uncomfortable.

"What do you know about Nick Murphy?" I ask.

Julian, confused and a touch hostile, says, "What do you mean, what do I know about Nick Murphy? Is that a trick question?"

"No, I mean, do you know if—" I'm suddenly sweating. "I mean—do you know if . . . if Murphy and Dakota were involved?"

Julian laughs, his lips cracking into a huge, ridiculous grin. Then: "Holy shit, you're serious?" He sobers up. "No. I mean, I don't know."

"He drives a yellow Bug."

"Murphy?"

"Yeah."

"He drives a Bug," he says to himself. Then, "What the fuck, he drives a *Bug*?"

We watch each other, disbelieving.

"What the hell does that even *mean*?"

"I don't know," I say. Because, truly, I don't.

174

· · ·

We're in Julian's Datsun. Then we're not.

"We're really doing this again?"

We're at Dakota's back door, knocking, not getting any response and breaking in with the spare key/fake rock.

"What now?"

We're upstairs.

"No effing idea," I say. "What the hell are we looking for this time?"

"I dunno." Julian's already digging through Dakota's desk drawers. "*Proof*, a clue—anything that links her to Murphy."

"Hey."

"Hmm?"

I stand still, watching him spin out. "Stop for a sec?"

"Why?" He checks his wristwatch. "We need to be quick, don't we? Emmett?"

"Just—for a second. Stop, please?" I bend for my bag, pulling Julian's binder notes from the front pocket. "I have something of yours."

"What?"

I pass the ball of crushed loose-leaf. He unravels it. His face fades to a tinny blue. "Why do you have this?"

"I'm sorry."

"Did you go through my shit?"

"I thought maybe—I just got freaked out. You left your

binder at my place and we'd just . . . I shouldn't have looked, I know, but I saw the letter, the apology . . ." He's blinking at me. *Bat, bat.* "You wrote that to yourself, right?" I'm babbling now. My ears are hot. "I thought maybe you'd done something . . ."

"Like what?"

". . . but now I know you didn't."

He sits down on Dakota's bed. "You thought I hurt her?"

"I—" I sit next to him. "I didn't know."

He takes a breath. Exhales. Takes another one. "You went through my shit."

"I'm really sorry."

"I would never hurt her."

I'm a jerk. A thief.

"I would never hurt *you*," he insists.

I let my fingers creep close to his thigh. Julian looks at me briefly, then gets up and starts searching again.

I get on my knees, check under the bed, pulling out and riffling through the same storage boxes I looked at last week. Thoughts of Dakota straddling Murphy flick through my brain, all of it in pornographic detail: after-school BJs, car sex, supply-closet hand jobs. What the hell happened between them? What did he *do* to her? Did they fight? Did she fuck up and threaten Gwen? Did he hit her too hard with something heavy and blunt, then toss her body off the sunshiney Santa Monica Pier?

"Christ."

Murphy? My preppy public-school god?

"Crap."

"What?" I whip back to life.

Julian is heaving, hunched over a teensy tower of textbooks. "This is pointless."

"Should we tell someone? The cops?"

"Tell them what? That our lit teacher drives a Volkswagen?" He tumbles back against the bed, breathlessly lighting his smoke.

"The cigarette . . . ?" I fan the air. "Emmett?"

"Dakota certainly won't mind." He inhales deep, exhales, shuts both eyes. "I just . . . I don't get it." I creep across the floor on hand and knee. He passes me his cigarette. "Why you?" he says.

"Me?" I ask, confused, dragging lightly on the squishy filter.

"Yeah," he says, rolling onto one hip, leaning sideways. "Why'd she call *you* and not me?"

"I—" I cough out some smoke and scrape my fingers through my hair. "I don't know," I say, suddenly guilty. "Wish I knew," I finish. I pass back the cigarette.

46.

Saturday.

Sam and I go to the river, which is less like a river and more like an empty cement ravine coiling through the city, valley to beach. We're walking. It's sunny. We pass people on horses. Written on a rock in red spray paint: *Raper*.

"Shouldn't it be *Rapist*?" I say to Sam.

He looks at the rock, at me; he smiles. "Your lit teacher called the house last night."

I freeze. Fear curls around my waist, binding me. "Why? Why the hell would he *call* you?"

"He says you've been pretty emotional. That you aren't turning in your work."

"I did—I *have*—that's complete horseshit. He has my *Jane* essay. He's refusing to read it—"

"Whoa, kid, it's okay. No one's reprimanding you. He

said you got a little weepy at school yesterday and he recommended"—he pulls a slip of paper from his wallet—"you make an appointment with this woman." He reads, "Griffith?"

"*Griffin.*"

"Right, her. He said to call her." He passes me the paper with *Griffin* written in messy cursive.

"I've already seen her. She didn't help."

"Adrienne, hey, just—do what the guy wants. Screw your head on straight. Get your grade up. It doesn't take much—"

"It's been a shit month."

"I know. I explained. I told him about Dakota."

"You did *what*?" Rising panic. "What did you tell him?"

"No, nothing. I said you knew her. That you were friends. That this—that this has been hard on you." He's watching me. "What's with you? Why is that bad?"

"Did you tell him about the car? About the Bug?"

His chin wrinkles. "Why would I tell him that?"

I relax. I say, "Sorry," and soften.

He blinks, eyeing me still. Kicks a wet rock. "Am I missing something?"

You're missing something, yes, only, "No," I say, instead. Surprising myself. "No, no—I'm being crazy."

I want to tell him everything, but am feeling stupidly superstitious. We're on the verge of something, me and

Julian. Saying this stuff out loud might, I don't know, cast some sort of jinx. Foil our dinky investigation.

"You're sure?" Sam asks, inspecting my face.

"I'm pissed about the paper," I tell him. "Murphy's been pressuring me and I—" I shake off a chill. "I cried about my paper."

47.

I'm on Lee's deluxe doorstep.

I used to love this place.

I loved how Lee lived like a Hollywood prince is his parents' opulent art deco home. I liked lying on silky couches and hiding behind heavy curtains, and I *loved* the way Lee legitimately valued his life. He wasn't one of those shitty kids who rolled around in piles of money, smoking French cigarettes and eating cocaine. He adored his parents and loved their home and he really, really appreciated life. Lee loved me. For a minute, I loved him. And then shit happened and I fucked it all up.

Ding, the bell. The door cracks. "Hi," I say. Lee lets me in.

We sit on the den sofa. I wonder if this is the last time I'll sit here watching the walls shimmer—all that shiny gold-leaf paper. "We're breaking up, right?"

"I kissed Alice Reed," he says.

"What, once?"

"Not just once."

I don't tell him about the things I did with Julian, because what would that matter now? "I figured," I say. "She called me. She's called me a bunch, actually."

"She's scared of you."

"Oh yeah?"

"She likes you."

"She *likes* me?"

"Sure."

I grimace. "She likes you better."

Lee smiles. I smile. Acting happy hurts. "I'm sorry for treating you like shit," I say.

Lee bobs his head. "Thanks."

I slide across the couch cushions and wind my arms around his neck. "I don't deserve you," I whisper, and Lee starts to vibrate. He's shaking like crazy and crying. "Hey, hey . . ." I coo.

"I don't need to be with her. I can be with you, still."

"I don't think you can," I say, and we cling to each other. Lee pulls his head back and kisses me.

48.

I'm awake.

It takes me fifteen seconds to realize that that chirpy bird melody is my phone. I switch on the bedside lamp and grab my cell off the nightstand. No freakin' number. Four a.m. *Fuck, Alice. Seriously?* I pick up.

"What now?"

Sobbing. Full-blown hysterical shrieks. The voice is high and broken and alarmingly familiar. It's not Alice. It says, "Adrienne?"

I shoot out of bed, fully freaked. I trip over my jeans, crumpled up in a ball on the floor. "Who *is* this?" I screech. My heart is all fast and screwy like a metronome off its beat.

"It's me," replies a thin, shaky voice from so very far away. "It's Dakota."

49.

"Sometimes I think—" She starts, then stops, hurling herself down onto the floor, next to me. "Don't you ever wonder what real love feels like?"

"Real love?"

"Yeah. Like really real love."

"I guess," I say, uneasy. "Sure." I pick at the berber carpet, pulling loose a few nylon loops.

"I never think about loving anyone. You think that's weird?"

"I—" I stiffen. "Never?"

"Not ever." She blinks. "I only ever think about people loving me."

I look at her perfect, poreless complexion. Her bony shoulders. Her puffy upper lip. "That dress looks better on you," I say.

She pulls her chin to her chest, looking down, assessing herself. "Does it?" she asks.

"Yes," I say. "It does."

She smiles. Then she cups my cheek with one hand and kisses me. She does it easily, with zero hesitation. She leans forward, her lips parting, and nudges my mouth with her mouth. I don't stop her. I don't ask where it's coming from or what the hell she means by it. I kiss back. Because maybe it feels nice or maybe I haven't been kissed enough. And who doesn't want to be wanted by her?

She moves closer. She sucks on my bottom lip and laughs. She takes my hand and sets it firmly on her breast. I jump a little, but leave it there. Then, abruptly, she pulls back. Swipes at her smeared lipstick. Says, coolly, "Everyone's the same. Boys, girls." She shakes her head, glaring. Then she gets up, grabs her coat and bag, and heads for the door.

"Where are you going?" I whisper, still on the ground.

"I told you. On my date." She's halfway down the hall already. She's not looking back.

50.

It's quarter to six, dark still, and Julian's doing ninety on the I-15. We haven't talked since LA. Dakota's three hours east, in some teensy desert town by Barstow. This is happening. I'm scratching and pinching at my thighs through my jeans because, yes, *this is totally real.*

Julian chews his nails to the quick. We blow smoke out open windows. Springsteen's "I'm on Fire" plays on repeat for a fourth of the trip, making me feel really sentimental and tense.

Half past seven. We're here. The sun creeps over a dry, jagged landscape. Julian parks the car in a dirt lot beside Dakota's motel. The place is sad—ten crumply units, side by side in one long row. Neon sign: "Vacancy. Free TV. Guest Laundry. No pets." For three full seconds I'm sick, then just as fast, I'm fine. I'm watching the moment, not in it. *You dump your boyfriend. You chase the dead girl.* Life in second person. Things are better this way.

We walk to unit four. Julian looks past me, hesitates, then knocks. We wait a bit. He knocks again. We wait some more. There's some clicking. The door rattles and cracks.

"Adrienne?" I see a sliver of nose first, shiny and thin. Then one wide eye.

"Can you undo the chain?"

She shuts the door. The lock scrapes. Then there she is, all of her: bare-faced, kid-like, wearing an oversize Bowie T-shirt. Her legs are bruised. She doesn't look like the real Dakota. *Mischievous. Cocksure.* She looks beaten and girlish. A bony pile of white skin and limp hair.

"I can't believe—" My relief is epic. I feel warm and loose. "I'm just so happy to see you."

She doesn't say anything back. Her eyes flick sideways, to Julian. "Why is he here?"

A whack to my gut. I look at sad, stiff Julian.

"I don't have a car," I say lamely. "And he cares about you."

She turns away, walks inside, hides herself. "Make him leave, please? I don't like the way I look."

I'd like to, like, repeatedly rip her face off.

Sorry, I mouth, facing Julian.

"I'll be in the car," he says flatly, and he's hurt, I see it, but he backs away. I follow Dakota inside.

187

Stained carpet. Orange, pilly bedspread. Kitchenette. TV. The place has a sweet, chemical smell that makes me spacey and nauseated. I beeline for the sink, grab two clear cups with a grayish tint off the bar, and fill them with tap water. Then I walk one over to Dakota.

"Here."

"Glad you came." She sips some water and pats the bed. Smiles wanly.

I sit, guzzling from my glass. The water tastes like pennies. "How long have you been here?" I ask, fitting the cup between my thighs. It's the first thing I think to say. *Where the fuck have you been?* seems too cruel and aggressive.

"A while."

"Doing what?"

She shrugs. Bends over. Picks up a half-eaten package of Red Vines. "Want some?"

No, I don't want some. I'm furious. Suddenly. It's a wild feeling—fierce, knotted, stuck just beneath my rib cage. "I don't," I whisper. *Red Vines?* Why the hell am I here? A month of misery, self-loathing, guilt—all for what? For *this*? Why is Julian stuck outside in the car? What sort of crappy creature can't even say, *hi, hello*, to her ex? Why've I spent weeks—no, *years*—obsessing over someone so totally hard-hearted and *fucked*? Why was I wearing her clothes, worshipping at her altar of rock? *Christ*, why'd I obliterate my relationship with Lee? I twist fully forward so she can't block me out. "Dakota."

She takes a tiny bite of licorice, mumbles, "Uh-huh?" She's chewing still, and rocking slightly. Pitching back and forth, her knees tucked under her sheer shirt.

"Are you high?"

"Don't be dumb."

Fuck you, fuck you, fuck OFF. I swallow a scream. "You know what people think back home, right? That you're dead. That you killed yourself."

She doesn't flinch, look up, change shades. She stays very much the same—pleasantly unresponsive.

"Do you know why?"

Another shrug.

"They found a note in your Jeep." And, "You made quite a splash."

She sighs heavily, gets up, picks a pair of jeans up off the floor, and slides them over her feet.

"Do you remember the last time we hung out?" I ask.

She looks at me, finally, fully connecting. "The guy who owns this place?" she says, switching subjects. "He cuts me a deal."

I can't help but wonder what he gets in exchange. "Oh yeah?"

"I couldn't afford it otherwise. I mean, it's a shit hole, but I'm broke."

Of course. "So that's why you called?"

"I don't want your money," she snaps, shifting her weight

from leg to leg. "I'm pregnant," she finishes, flatly.

My gut flops.

"I mean, I *was*. I'm not now." She follows fast with, "It wasn't Julian's, if that's what you're thinking."

I was and I wasn't. "I'm sorry," I say, but do I mean it? Am I surprised?

"It's fine," she offers. "I didn't lose it or anything. I came here to have it but I just—I couldn't—*can't* be a mom."

I nod slowly, the picture crystallizing. "Were you . . . was it Murphy?" I ask.

She stares for a bit, then smiles, and I see a glimmer of old Dakota. "He make a pass at you?"

"What? *No*."

She drops down into a chair, tugging boots on over jeans. "Nick—he likes little girls." Wow. "He liked *me*, anyways. I think maybe—" She pauses to chew a cuticle. "Maybe I loved him. You think that's possible? That I loved him?"

"How would I know?"

"He never said it back." More candy. "He talked about the baby a lot. Not ours." She looks up. "The one he was having with Gwen." Then, real casual: "Did she have it yet? Her kid?"

"Yeah."

"What is it?"

"A girl."

She blinks. Blinks more.

I wait a moment. "What about the jacket?" I ask.

"Hmm?"

"The army jacket," I say. "With the writing."

She perks up. "Oh, my jacket? Oh yeah. Why, what about it?"

"We just, we thought—" I stop, starting again: "What's with the numbers?"

"Oh." She wrinkles her nose.

"I mean, they're dates, right?"

She shrugs.

"Just—can you *not* be coy right now?"

"Right, yes, they're dates."

"Marking what?"

"Just . . . days . . ." *Spit. It. Out.* ". . . I was with Nick." She squirms. "You know. Like, *biblically*."

Holy fuck, she sucks. *He* sucks. They've been fucking around for *years*. Since sophomore year. "You're serious?"

"Of course, yes."

"Well, what about your *boyfriend*?"

"Jesus, Adrienne. We were never official. I never committed. Not really, anyways."

"He says something different."

"Of course he does. Of *course*. He's, like, rewriting history. He wanted it that way, he did, but I was never—" She shakes her head. "I wasn't ever really . . . free."

I picture Julian outside, alone. My chest tightens. "You left that note," I say.

"Note?"

"In your Jeep."

"Oh. That." She tilts her head. "Well, I wanted to do this. For real. Start over. But, you know . . . I thought it would feel different, being on my own."

"Like how?"

"Like, *good*. Like I'd raise my kid and make money off music and I'd be, I dunno, happy. Don't you ever just want to be *new*?"

I look down at my grubby jeans. I get a quick flash of Julian. Then of Lee back home with Alice Reed. I think of Dakota's dress crumpled up in that dumpster. "Yeah," I say. "Sometimes I want to be new."

She slides sideways off the chair. "How much shit am I in?"

"Sorry?"

"At home. If you take me back now, how fucked am I, really?"

"I don't . . ." I trail off. "Not sure."

"I'm screwed, right? God, I can't—"

"You *can*," I interject thoughtlessly. I have no clue what sort of trouble she'll face—legally, socially—but none of that matters now, does it? She's broke, alone, miserable, friendless.

"Yeah, *and*? What happens then?"

She'll worm free, won't she? She's manipulative, shrewd, charismatic, self-serving—

"I come back, and what?"

"I—" I clam up. She's pale and meek without makeup, and for a split second I feel bigger and better than: I have a home, a Kate, a mom, a Sam. What does she have?

"Do you even like me?" she asks, a tiny tug in her voice.

"I—" *Do* I? I've spent four weeks obsessively mooning and grieving, and now here she is—she's real, she's here, she's disappointingly small. I think back to that last exchange, sophomore year, in my room. My dress, her date, *I only ever think about people loving me.* "I don't know," I admit. "Not really."

She nods. "That's fine," she says, then, "Take me back?"

"Okay," I say. I get up.

51.

It's everywhere now. *Teen faked her own suicide.* It's all over the papers, the local news; it's all anyone at school can talk about (*'twas drugs, a psychotic break, extreme narcissism, borderline tendencies*). Of course, the real "whys," the meaty details, Dakota keeps to herself. She's home again, with Emmett, and I'm back at school trying to pull my shit together. Julian's MIA, but I'm not thinking about him right now. I'm not thinking of *her*, either.

"Bat-shit, right?" It's Kate, at my side suddenly.

"Hmm?"

"Oh, puhleaze. Like you know nothing. You and band boy. You want?" She offers up half her candy bar. "Salty chocolate. All the rage." I take the foil packet. "You feel like telling me any D. Webb deets? I know you know stuff."

"I do." I break off a piece of chocolate. Nibble at it. The earth, literally, shakes.

"Seriously?" Kate shrieks, sliding sideways toward the

restroom. Shit's rumbling. Lockers bang. Everyone scatters, laughing nervously—clinging to each other, the doorways and walls, rocking.

"*Hate, hate, hate* this . . ." I whisper, squeezing Kate's hand. She squeezes back. Three seconds later:

Loud, enthusiastic applause. Cheering. A few whoots. "It's over." Kate steps away from the wall. "See? Tiny quake. So nothing."

"I gotta go outside," I say, suddenly sweaty.

"You okay?"

"Fine."

I'm backing up, turning away, jogging quickly toward the exit.

Lee's favorite spot. Rocks, cacti, school pool.

I'm pacing, clutching my hot chest, trying to calm the fuck down. Panic attack. It's happened before. Once, while stuck at a light at the Glendale-Alvarado intersection in Echo Park; another time, on the 110 north with Sam driving.

This time it's that same creepy buildup: I'm shaky and tingly and can't keep still. Like some vicious, upside-down orgasm. Someone passes by and asks if I'm all right. I must look insane—pacing, *weeping*. I wave the guy away and pull a pack of Altoids from my book bag. I chew two. It helps, eating something—whips me back to earth.

52.

"Hi."

I'm standing in Murphy's doorway. He's hunched over a stack of papers.

"Hello, hello?" I repeat.

He jumps, looking up. "Adrienne, wow, hey." He's clutching his chest and grinning uneasily. "You scared me."

"Did I?" I lean against the door, snapping it shut with one hip bump.

"Everything okay?"

I've never seen the guy so manic and jerky. I shuffle forward and drop down in front of his desk. "Sure."

"Crazy quake, right?"

"Right."

He smiles. Does his signature head rub. Back to front, *rub, rub, rub.*

I feel a flicker of that earlier panic: zippy heart, dizziness. "I came to tell you something," I blurt.

"Oh?"

News of Dakota's miraculous resurrection broke yesterday, but I can't tell if the waxy glaze in his eyes spells relief or big terror.

"Yes," I say, feeling really ridiculous. This—whatever *this* is (some sort of showdown? Face-off?)—smacks of utter BS. I'm playing dress up. Faking it. "I'm dropping your class," I tell him.

His gaze narrows. "You can't *drop* lit, Adrienne. It's not an elective."

"Right, no, I know." I pick at some paint peeling off the lip of his wood desk. "I just—" My tongue is sandpaper dry. "I think—" *I'm doing this. I'm really, really doing this.* "I think you're gonna pass me. You're gonna mark me on time and here *every day*, and then I don't have to—" *Say it, Adrienne, for fuck's sake, FINISH it.* "I don't have to watch you lie like a rat anymore."

His lips part. Out seeps a thin, two-syllable moan.

"You're not a family man," I say. "You're not some upstanding, shiny, clean guy."

"Adrienne—"

"You're a lech." My voice quivers like some brooding soap star. "I know what you did, okay? And I know who you did it with."

197

He stays very still, caught, yellow, his Adam's apple bobbing.

"So. To reiterate: I'm dropping lit. And you get to keep
your job. And, ya know, your *kid* and your *marriage*." I stand,
feeling triumphant and massively freaked out.

"Adrienne, come on, s-sit down," he stammers. "Let's
just—let's *talk*, okay?"

"I don't want to talk to you."

"Adrienne—"

"I'm done," I say, swinging my book bag over one shaky
shoulder. And, "We good?"

He leans back. Drops his pen. Rubs his head the wrong
way (front to back). "Yes," he says, acquiescing. "We're good."

53.

I find Kate later. After school, by her car. She's pressed against the driver's-side door, something big and dark mauling her body. My first impulse? To attack, claw at, *kill* the creature sucking her face off, but—wait—they're *kissing*. *Mashing. Loving*, not fighting. I jog ten feet closer and crouch by Kate's front left wheel. I'm trying for a better view of the assailant: dark coat, big boots, likes to yank ponytails and bite earlobes:

Wyatt Earp.

I let go an involuntary yelp of glee. Kate pulls back, twists around, wipes her mouth. "Knox?"

"Hi," I whisper. "Hi, sorry, carry on." I stand up. "I'll come back."

"No, Knox, I'm driving you home." She turns to Wyatt, says softly, "I'm driving her home."

"That's cool."

Their grins are gooey. They love each other. *Oh my god they love each other.* "Bye." More smooching. More pawing each other's faces. Wyatt looks longingly at Kate while backing away. He says, "Later, Knox."

I wave. Wait a beat. Kate pushes away from her car and whips around. I pounce. "What the fuuuuuuuuuuck??!!!!"

She winks. "What? No big thang."

"You liar! You lie, you lie, you *lie*! You love him."

"I don't."

"Oh gosh, you *love* him!"

"Stop." She pushes my head down, checking over one shoulder to see where Wyatt's gone.

I lean in, sniff her neck. "You smell like boy."

"Fuck off." She slaps at me. "Get in the car."

I do. She does. We look at each other. "How the hell did this happen?" I say.

"Thanks."

"No, I mean—" I think about it. "No, actually, that's exactly what I mean. What the fuck, *how*?"

"He's shy," Kate says plainly. "He needed encouragement."

"The letter?"

"The letter, sure. I texted too."

"Saying what?"

"I asked him to come over."

"You made out with him."

She laughs. "Right, *I* made out with him."

"You *did*, right? You totally had to kiss *him*?"

"Oh, absolutely."

"What's wrong with dudes?"

"So much."

We're beaming.

"You ready?"

I nod, buckling up. We exit the student lot, gliding by faculty and backed-up yellow busses, rolling past clusters of frosh Dakota wannabes looking upbeat and chipper. Then, Christ, there's Lee with Alice Reed on the curb, ready to cross, clutching hands. "Crap," Kate mumbles, and all my joy leaks out my feet. "You okay?"

We drive by. Lee grins warmly, waves. I nod back. "Fine," I say to Kate, looking forward, a smidge queasy.

"You sure?"

I'm pissed at myself. Feeling regretful and confused, but also? Unashamedly free. I smile at Kate just to see if it sticks.

"Pretty," she says.

"Thank you."

"You want to eat something? Smoke something? We don't have to go home yet."

I watch out the window. Kate's shiny palms. Jewish deli in the distance. "Drop me someplace?"

"Yeah, anywhere. Where you wanna go?"

54.

I ding the bell. Kate watches from the street, her car softly rumbling. Dakota answers, looking more like herself than she did two days ago, wearing a knee-length witchy dress, and over that, a thin violet hoodie.

"Adrienne."

I whirl around and wave good-bye to Kate, who waves back. Then say, "Can I come in?"

We sit side by side on her sofa. A clean pile of laundry stacked on Emmett's recliner. Something moody and acoustic playing on the stereo. Angry piano. Smoky girl vocals.

"Where's Emmett?"

"Work."

I watch the rug, the window, the wall clock. She doesn't offer more, and I wonder what their relationship looks like now, post–Dakota desert retreat.

"Did you want anything?" she asks, picking at a thumb-nail. "Juice? Coke?"

I shake my head. Ask if she's feeling okay.

"Fine," she says quietly. She looks alert, antsy. She waits for it:

"I need to know something," I say.

"Yeah?"

"That phone call." I'm shifting in place. "Before you left—that message."

"What about it?"

"Why me?"

"Why you *what*?"

"We hadn't talked in years."

Dakota wiggles around, then deflects with, "You and Julian getting along all right?"

I flinch, look down at my pale hands. "We're just friends."

"No you're not." The CD skips. I glance up. She's half smiling, shrugging one shoulder. "It's okay. He's a good guy. He needs someone nice, like you."

I wave dismissively. Guilty. Caught.

"Anyways," she continues, cheerfully redirecting our talk. "I don't know why I called." A beat. "I felt bad. Thought you might pick up."

I pick a set of socks off Emmett's recliner—roll them into a snug ball, then set them back down. "What'd you feel bad about?"

"What do you mean?"

"You said you *felt* bad."

She pauses as if to retrace her wording. "I meant, yeah, I meant what I said. It feels shitty not having friends."

"You had friends."

"Who?"

"Your band? Julian? You have legions of obsessed freshman girls *dying* to get close to you."

"They're not my friends," she says. "I've seen you with that girl."

"Kate?"

"The one that dropped you off?"

I nod.

"It's nice, the way you are together. We were never like that, were we?"

Something hard and sharp solidifies in my heart. "No," I say. "We weren't." She's *lonely*. Of course. Years of pushing people sideways, of manipulation and seduction and worthless, sexy gestures—a wink, a lick—then what? Who's left now? "Why'd we stop talking?" I ask.

Her face falls. She crosses her ankles and clasps her hands like someone so virtuous and good. "I stopped liking you."

I swallow my shock. My belly—instantly rigid.

"You just—you let me *do* things to you," she continues. "Everything was always so easy. You were like a boy—super agreeable and passive and doting."

She's right. I let her lead, always. She told me who to like and what to wear and how to play.

"I stopped respecting you." Her voice trembles a bit. Her mouth settles into a straight, unreadable line. "I wanted something, I dunno, mutual, I guess? And what we had? Nothing was ever *even*."

"So . . ." I see it now—all her faulty, fucked-up logic. "That was a test, that kiss? You were *testing* me?"

She rolls her bottom lip between her pointer finger and thumb. "I don't know."

"Sure you do." It's her party trick. Seduce anyone! Your teacher, your bandmate, your best friend. "Anyone's fuckable, right?"

She glares back. "Right."

I stand up, hot with fury. "You're insane."

"No, I'm *right*."

"About *what*?"

"All anyone wants? Is to have their pretty, precious ego stroked." She's standing now. "No one wants anything real."

"That's stupid."

"It's true."

"You? You're not real."

"Right. No, I know. I'm the fantasy."

"You set *traps*."

"Yes! I do! And you *all always fail*."

I sit down, hands on head. Take three slow breaths. Pat

my hair. "I wanted you to like me." My voice breaks. *"You
never seemed like you liked me."*

"I did."

"Oh yeah? What'd you like about me?"

She laughs. "Can't remember."

I turn away, toward the wall. "I remember what I liked
about you."

"Oh yeah?"

"Yeah."

"Well?"

"You were fun. For a while." I cluck my tongue. "You were
really, really fun."

She's quiet for a bit. "You think I don't see anyone but
myself."

I shrug.

Then, softly, as if whispering to a puppy or a child, "Hey,
turn around." She touches my shoulder. "Hey, come on. I
won't bite."

I don't believe her. I twist forward.

"People like me for the wrong reasons."

"Meaning?" I say, my patience waning.

She sighs heavily. "They want to screw me. Or *know* me.
They like my music. They like the way I look." Her voice is
flat. "My songs, my clothes—none of that's me."

I consider this. *Recognize it.* Me in Dakota's dresses,
smoking her cigarettes, wearing her eyeliner. Lee wanting

me. Me hating him for it. "I get it," I say, because suddenly, unexpectedly, I do.

Dakota slouches, relaxing slightly.

"But you make it that way, you know that, right? You invite it," I say. "You don't get to—" I stop, searching for the right analogy. "—put up a sign selling fruit"—*lame*—"then get pissed when people want to buy apples off you."

She blinks. Picks up the remote. Puts it back down. "I guess," she says softly, and the mood lifts a little. "How'd you meet Kate?"

"Ceramics. Sophomore year. She and Lee—they were kind of, like, a package deal."

She looks at me. "Where's Lee now?"

"We broke up."

"Right, Julian."

"Nothing's happening with Julian—"

She makes a face.

"Well, I don't know," I say quickly, defensively. I look at the wall clock: 4:12. I look outside: nearly dark.

"I used to see you guys by the pool sometimes between periods. You and Lee."

"Yeah. We liked it there."

"You seemed happy."

"We were," I say, blotting my runny nose with my sweater sleeve. "I fucked it up."

"Yeah?"

"Yeah," I say, nodding.

"Well." Dakota shrugs. "I relate. I fuck shit up all the time."

Right. At least I don't fake suicides and fuck a billion people and break hearts and set traps. I suppress a giggle.

"Go ahead, laugh," she says, pulling a Red Vine loose from an open package on the coffee table. "It's funny. *I'm* funny," she says, laughing now too. Chewing and sucking and rolling her eyes.

55.

Elysian Park, two thirty, Saturday.

Green trees. Brown grass. Men in white vans.

I'm waiting for Julian.

It's breezy and crisp. There're a gazillion dogs off leash. I used to come here all the time with Sam on hikes. We stopped a few years ago when we discovered the reservoir: flatter, less sketchy, just as many dogs but more babies in strollers.

I missed this. Eastside wilderness. Overgrown and a little grimy.

"Hi."

Two thirty-two. Here he is. "Hey."

"You ready?"

I nod and climb over the rusty guardrail.

"Haven't been here in forever," he says.

"Me neither."

"Nice, right?"

"Totally."

We stand at the base of the hill together, staring up.

"Steep."

"Yep."

"You have an okay week?" I ask. "You were out sick."

"I wasn't, really. I was just—home." Of course. Dakota fallout. She's back. He's reeling. He sticks a hand out. "Tired already. Help me up?"

I take his fingers, yanking hard. They're dry and hot, and touching him gives me the nuttiest little thrill. We run together, huffing, for a hard fifteen seconds. Then we rest, hunched over, inhaling and exhaling like old, fat men.

"What?" he says. A crooked look.

It's different, being with him. Things feel bright now, less dirty and sad. He looks the same, only shades pinker. No Dakota lens skewing my view.

"We don't really know each other," I hear myself say.

"No," he says, righting himself. "I guess we don't."

We're walking again.

"I went a little crazy this month."

"Oh yeah?"

"I don't really smoke, you know."

"Yeah, you make shitty smoke rings."

I smile, hands on hips, leaning into the incline. "I was an asshole to Lee," I say. Lee. Who's on his third official day of *doing* Alice Reed. "Super shitty," I mumble. They get four full weeks of supper club—free of me—we agreed. Seems only fair. "Have you seen Dakota?" I ask. Julian's watching the ground, not me.

"Wednesday. I had some stuff of hers I wanted to get rid of."

Rid of. I relax, slightly. Still: "Happy to have her back?"

He frowns. "Happy she's safe." After a beat: "We're done, Dakota and me. You know that, right?" His brow scrunches up. "I mean, the whole screwing-my-lit-teacher thing . . . ?"

I laugh. Can't help it. Psychotic relief.

"Hey, look." He points.

We've plateaued. Beneath us, a deep, empty ravine. A runner and two dogs jog past, collars and keys jingling.

"It's all downhill," he says. There's a wonky, unhinged feeling in my chest. I look at my sneakers, powdered with gritty, gray dust. "Hey."

"Hmm?"

"I—"

I kiss him. Super quick. Then, bouncing backward, I blurt, "Just checking."

He laughs. "Checking *what*? My vitals?"

"Checking, you know, to see if . . ." I shut my eyes. Shake my head. *Jesus, Adrienne.* "To see if—" I'm whispering. "To see if I feel the same."

"Well?" he says, amused. "What's the verdict?"

I look at him. "Yeah, you know." I shrug. "You still got it."

We do it again.

This time, though, we go slow. His hands slide around my ribs. I get a chill.

"Gimme your hand," he says. I do, I give him my hand.

"You ready? Let's run for it."

"Okay," I say, gazing downward, my pulse quickening with something girlish and crazy-making—adrenaline? Hope?

"Count of three." He squeezes my fingers. I squeeze back—"One, two"—then let go, darting ahead. I'm flying, flailing, screaming gleefully all the way down.

"Adrienne, wait!"

I don't. I scream louder. My heels pound the sandy ground and something mystifying and joyful creeps high up my spine.

acknowledgments

Anica Rissi and Jen Rofé, I am so stupidly lucky to have you two in my life. Thank you both for your support, wisdom, enthusiasm, faith, and friendship.

Pulse team, endless thanks, as always, for all you do.

Jade Chang, Adeline Colangelo, Amanda Yates, Milly Sanders, Jenna Blough, Anna Spanos, Morgan Matson, Hannah Moskowitz—massive gratitude for your feedback and writerly guidance.

Joanna Weinberg Lawless, you know how you helped. Thank you. Love you.

Dad and Aaron, thanks for being the absolute best.

"You think he's yours but he's not," I thought.
"You think he's yours but really he's mine."

Lauren Strasnick

NOTHING LIKE YOU

"Candid and quick-paced, with characters you can't help but want the best for."
—DEB CALETTI, National Book Award Finalist

TURN THE PAGE FOR A PEEK AT
LAUREN STRASNICK'S
NOTHING LIKE YOU

Chapter 1

We were parked at Point Dume, Paul and I, the two of us tangled together, half dressed, half not. Paul's car smelled like sea air and stale smoke, and from his rearview hung a yellow and pink plastic lanyard that swayed with the breeze drifting in through the open car window. I hung on to Paul, thinking, *I like your face, I love your hands, let's do this, let's do this, let's do this,* one arm locked around the back of his head, the other wedged between two scratched-up leather seat cushions, bracing myself against the pain while wondering, idly, if this feels any different when you love the person or when you do it lying down on a bed.

This was the same beach where I'd spent millions of mornings with my mother, wading around at low tide searching for sea anemone and orange and purple starfish. It had cliffs and crashing waves and seemed like the appropriate place to do something utterly unoriginal, like lose my virginity in the backseat of some guy's dinged-up, bright red BMW.

I didn't really know Paul but that didn't really matter. There we were, making sappy, sandy memories on the Malibu Shore, fifteen miles from home. It was nine p.m. on a school night. I needed to be back by ten.

"That was nice," he said, dragging a hand down the back of my head through my hair.

"Mm," I nodded, not really sure what to say back. I hadn't realized the moment was over, but there it was—our unceremonious end. "It's getting late, right?" I dragged my jeans over my lap. "Maybe you should take me home?"

"Yeah, absolutely," Paul shimmied backward, buttoning his pants. "I'll get you home." He wrinkled his nose, smiled, then swung his legs over the armrest and into the driver's side seat.

"Thanks," I said, trying my best to seem casual and upbeat, hiking my underwear and jeans back on, then creeping forward so we were seated side by side.

"You ready?" he asked, pinching an unlit cigarette between his bottom and top teeth.

"Sure thing." I buckled my seat belt and watched Paul run the head of a Zippo against the side seam on his pants, igniting a tiny flame. I turned my head toward the window and pressed my nose against the glass. There, in the not-so-far-off distance, an orange glow lit the sky, gleaming bright. *Brushfire.*

"Remind me, again?" He jangled his car keys.

"Hillside. Off Topanga Canyon."

"Right, sorry." He lit his cigarette and turned the ignition. "I'm shit with directions."

Chapter 2

Topanga was burning.

Helicopters swarmed overhead dumping water and red glop all over fiery shrubs and mulch. The air tasted sour and chalky and my eyes and throat burned from the blaze. Flaming hills, thick smoke—this used to seriously freak me out. Now, though, I sort of liked it. My whole town tinted orange and smelling like barbecue and burnt pine needles.

I was standing in my driveway, Harry's leash wrapped twice around my wrist. We watched the smoke rise and billow behind my house and I thought: *This is what nuclear war must look like. Mushroom clouds and raining ash.* I bent down, kissed Harry's dry nose, and scratched hard behind his ears. "One quick walk," I said. "Just down the hill and back."

He barked.

We sped through the canyon. Past tree swings and chopped wood and old RVs parked on lawns. Past the plank bridge that crosses the dried-out ravine, the Topanga Christian Fellowship with its peeling blue and white sign, the Christian Science Church, the Topanga Equestrian Center with the horses on the hill and the fancy veggie restaurant down below in their shadow. That day, the horses were indoors, shielded from the muddy, smoky air. Harry and I U-turned at the little hippie gift shop attached to the fancy veggie restaurant, and started back up the hill to my house.

Barely anyone was out on the road. It was dusky out, almost dark, so we ran the rest of the way home. I let Harry off his leash once we'd reached my driveway, then followed him around back to The Shack.

"Knock, knock," I said, rattling the flimsy tin door and pushing my way in. Nils was lying on his side reading an old issue of *National Geographic*. I kicked off my sneakers and dropped Harry's leash on the ground, flinging myself down next to Nils and onto the open futon.

"Anything good?" I asked, grabbing the magazine from between his fingertips.

"Fruit bats," he said, grabbing it back.

I shivered and rolled sideways, butting my head against his back.

"You cold?" he asked.

"No," I said. "Just a chill . . ."

He rolled over and looked at me. My eyes settled on his nose: long and straight and reassuring. "You freaked about the fire?" he asked.

I shrugged.

"They've got it all pretty much contained, you know. 'Least last time I checked."

I grabbed a pillow off the floor and used it to prop up my head. Harry was sniffing around at my toes, licking and nibbling at my pinkie nail. I laughed.

"What?" said Nils. "What's so funny?"

"Just Harry." I shook my head.

"No, come on, what?"

I grabbed his magazine back. "Fruit bats," I squealed, holding open the page with the fuzzy flying rodents. "I want one, okay? This year, for my birthday."

"Sure thing, princess." He moved closer to me, curling his legs to his chest. "Anything you say."

Nils is my oldest friend. My next-door neighbor. This shack has been ours since we were ten. It was my dad's toolshed for about forty-five minutes—before Nils and I met, and took over. The Shack is its new name, given a ways back on my sixteenth birthday. Years ten through fifteen, we called it Clubhouse. Nils thought The Shack sounded much more grown up. I agree. The Shack has edge.

"Have you done all your reading for Kiminski's quiz tomorrow?"

"No" I said, flipping the page.

"Where were you last night, anyway? I came by but Jeff said you were out."

Jeff is my dad, FYI. "I just went down to the beach for a bit."

"Alone?" Nils asked.

"Yeah, alone," I lied, dropping Nils's magazine and flipping onto my side.

Nils didn't need to know about Paul Bennett or any other boy in my life. Nils had, at that point, roughly five new girlfriends each week. I'd stopped asking questions.

"Hols, should we study?"

"Put on Jethro Tull for two secs. We can study in a bit." The weeks prior to this Nils and I had spent sorting through my mother's entire music collection, organizing all her old records, tapes, and CDs into categories on a shelf Jeff had built for The Shack.

"This song sucks," shouted Nils over the first few bars of "Aqualung." I raised one hand high in the air, rocking along while scanning her collection for other tapes we might like.

"Hols?"

"Yeah?"

"Your mom had shit taste in music."

I squinted. "You *so* know you love it. Admit it. You *love* Jethro Tull."

"I do. I love Jethro Tull." He was looking at me. His eyes looked kind of misty. *Don't say it, Nils, please don't say it.* "I miss your mom." He said it.

I sat up. "Buck up, little boy. She's watching us from a happy little cloud in the sky, okay?"

He tugged at my hair. "How come you never get sad, Holly? I think it's weird you don't ever get sad."

"I *do* get sad." I stood, dusting some dirt off my butt. "Just because you don't see it doesn't mean it isn't there."

Chapter 3

School.

7:44 a.m. and I was rushing down the hall toward World History with my coffee sloshing everywhere and one lock of sopping wet hair whipping me in the face. I got one "Hey," and two or three half-smiles from passersby right before sliding into my seat just as the bell went *ding ding ding*.

Ms. Stein was set to go with her number two pencil, counting heads, ". . . sixteen, seventeen . . . who's missing? Saskia? You here? Has anyone seen Saskia?" As if on cue, Saskia Van Wyck came racing through the door, *clickity-clack* in her shiny black flats, plopping down in the empty seat to my left. "I'm here, sorry! I'm right here," she said, dragging the back of her hand dramatically across her brow. *Adorable.* I slurped my coffee.

"Take out your books, people. Let's read until eight fifteen, then we'll discuss chapters nine and ten. 'Kay?"

I pulled my book from my bag and glanced to my left.

Saskia Van Wyck. Paul Bennett's girlfriend-slash-ex-girlfriend. I barely knew her. I only knew that she was skinny, pretty, marginally popular, and lived in this old adobe house just off the PCH, wedged right in between my favorite Del Taco and the old crappy gas station on Valley View Drive. I'd been there once, in sixth grade, for a birthday party, where no more than four kids showed up, but I remembered things: her turquoise blue bedroom walls. An avocado tree. A naked Barbie and a stuffed brown bear she kept hidden under her twin wrought-iron bed.

Saskia leaned toward me. "Do you have a highlighter or a pen or something I could borrow?"

"Yeah, okay." I reached into the front pocket of my backpack and pulled out a mechanical pencil. "How's this?" Suddenly I had a flash of that chart they show you in tenth-grade Sex Ed—How STDs Spread: *Billy sleeps with Kim who sleeps with Bobby who does it to Saskia who really gives it to Paul who sleeps with Holly, which makes Holly a big whore-y ho-bag who's slept with the entire school.*

"That's great," said Saskia, smiling. "Thanks."

I nodded and smiled back.

• • •

"Holly, move downstage a bit—to your left. And try your line again."

"Once more, with feeling," I deadpanned, closing my eyes and letting my head fall forward. *Gosh, I'm so clever.*

I walked downstage and shuffled sideways. "Wait—from where?"

"Start with: 'O, the more angel she, / And you the blacker devil!' And Desdemona, stay down—you're dead, remember?" Desdemona, or Rachel Bicks, who'd been sitting Indian-style on the stage sucking a Tootsie Pop, rolled her eyes and slinked back down. "Look more dead," Mr. Ballanoff barked. "Okay. Emilia, Othello. Go."

"'O, the more angel she, / And you the blacker devil!'"

"There's the spirit." Ballanoff turned toward Pete Kennedy, my scene partner, who was standing stage right holding a pillow. "Othello?"

Pete did his thing, kicking around the stage like an over-zealous mummy—he was big into *gesturing* and, somehow, still, he seemed so stiff. I *blah-blahed* back, just trying to keep my words straight without flubbing my lines. I don't think we'd made it through half the scene before Ballanoff was waving his clipboard, recklessly, *suddenly*, interjecting, "God, both of you, stop, please." Then, "Holly, god, come'ere."

I walked forward. "What? What's wrong now?"

"Where's the *fire*? He's just killed someone you love, he's calling her a whore—*where's the fire*, Holly?"

I shifted back and forth from leg to leg. "I ate too much at lunch. I'm tired. We only have three more minutes of class left. . . ."

He mashed his lips together, exhaling loudly, out his nose.

Ballanoff is Jeff's age about, early forties, but I've always thought he looked older than my dad until this year when Jeff aged ten years in a blink; going from salt and pepper to stark white in three months.

"All of you," Ballanoff shouted, "Learn your lines this week. Please. Work on feeling something *other* than apathy. Next class I expect changes." He smiled then, his eyes crinkling. "You can go."

I snatched my knapsack off the auditorium floor and lunged for the door.

"Holly."

"Yes?" I whipped around.

"Help me carry this stuff, will you?"

I trudged back down the aisle, grabbing a stack of books off a chair. Ballanoff took the other stack and together we walked out the theater doors, toward his office.

"How's your dad?" he asked, balancing his papers and books between his hands and chin.

"Fine. The same."

Ballanoff knew my mom in high school. They once sang a duet together from *Brigadoon*.

"How's Nancy?" I asked. Ballanoff's wife.

"Good, thanks." He unlocked his office door, kicked an empty cardboard box halfway across the room, then dumped the pile of books onto his cluttered desk.

I set my stack down on the floor next to the door. All four corners of his office were crammed with crooked piles of books, plays, and wrinkled papers. A tiny, blue recycling bin shoved against the wall was filled to its brim with empty diet Snapple bottles.

Ballanoff sighed, walked over to the mini fridge, and took out an iced tea. "I expect more from you."

"Yeah, I know."

"It wouldn't kill you to get a little angry, or to feel something real for a change." He paused for a bit, then said, "How are you, anyways?"

"Dreamy."

"That good, huh?" He collapsed into his black pleather desk chair, swiveling from side to side.

"Oh, yeah. Pep rallies and bonfires galore. Senior year really lives up to the fantasy."

He laughed, which made me happy, momentarily. "What about you?" I asked.

"What about me?"

"You know. How's life in the teachers' lounge?"

"Oh, hey." He took a long pull off his diet iced tea. "Same old shit, year after year."

I flashed my teeth. "I love it when you swear."

"I should watch it, right? Before Harper finds out and fires me for teaching curse words alongside *Othello*." Harper. Our principal.

"It's true. Look out. You're a danger, Mr. B."

"I should hope so." He slid two fingers over the lip of his wood desk. "Thanks for your help, Holly."

I perssed the sole of my sneaker against his shiny orange door. "Anytime."

"Tell Jeff hi for me, okay?"

"Will do." I pushed backward then, out of his office and back down the hall.

"Jesus, Nils, watch the windows."

Nils was all over some dumb girl, backing her into my driver-side car door, his grubby little fingertips pressed against the glass.

"Oh. Hi Hols, hey."

"Hi. *Move*, please."

He and the girl pushed sideways so I could get my key in the lock. "Much obliged."

The girl giggled and turned toward me. *Oh, no. Not her.*

"Hey, Hols? You know Nora . . ." Nora Bittenbender. From my Calc class. Before Nils she'd supposedly slept with two teachers: David Epstein and Rick Hyde. Pretty girl but *way* bland for my taste. Fair and freckled with these jiggly, big pale boobs she was always jamming into push-up bras and too-tight tank tops. Her weight fluctuated nonstop—skinny one week, chubs the next—and her taste, Jesus, *seriously question-able.* School ensembles that bounced between cheesy night-club clothes and oversized, heather-gray sweats. *Sexy.*

"Do you want a ride or not?" The hood of my car was covered in ash. I slid a finger through the dusty gray soot, then hopped inside. "I promised Jeff I'd take Harry out for a run after school, so either get in or I'm leaving."

"Right, yes! Okay." Nils ran over to the passenger-side door. Nora trailed him, holding on to the back of his shirt. "But could you drop Nora off on the way? She lives right by us, on Pawnee Lane."

No. "That's fine," I said. "Get in."

Nils crept into the backseat. Nora took shotgun. "Holly, thanks," she said. "I missed my bus."

"Yup."

"We have gym together, don't we?"

"Calc," I said, flooring the accelerator and, three seconds into my drive, nearly crashing into pedestrian Paul Bennett. *Good one, Holly.* I pulled to a stop and rolled down my window.

"Crap." He looked really great. He was wearing this old, thin, button-down with a small tear at the collar. His bangs lay on a diagonal across his forehead, hitting his eyes just so. "You missed me by a millimeter!"

"I'm sorry! I'm *so* sorry! Are you okay?"

Paul started toward my window, then, spotting Nils and Nora, stopped short and readjusted his backpack. "I'm fine. Just"—he waved his hands in the air and smiled—"startled, is all."

"Right. Sorry."

I watched his hair blow backward as he turned and walked on toward his car. Then I lightly pushed down on the gas and rolled out onto the main road.

"I didn't even know you knew Paul Bennett." Nils had scooched forward in his seat so that his face was floating somewhere over my armrest.

"I don't, not really."

"You sure? 'Cause he seems to know you."

I felt something un-nameable tickle my gut. Regret? Longing? I shook my head. "I mean, we have a class together. He knows my name, I guess."

"Maybe he likes you," said Nora, poking me in the shoulder.

Nils scoffed. "No offense, but, I don't think Holly's really Paul Bennett's type."

"What's that supposed to mean?" I turned sideways and gave Nils the icy eyeball. "What's Paul Bennett's type? Please! Pray tell."

Nils folded a stick of cinnamon gum into his mouth. "You know, blond. Willowy. WASPy. The anti-Holly."

"Saskia Van Wyck," said Nora, nodding.

I rolled my eyes. "Of course. Saskia Van Wyck, the anti-Holly."

"That's a good thing, Hols. She's plain spaghetti." He looked at me lovingly. "No sauce."

Nora twisted around in her seat so that she was facing Nils. "Can I have a piece of that?" She was biting Nils on the neck and pulling on his pack of gum. "I *love* cinnamon. I do."

We spent the next twenty minutes stuck in traffic on the PCH. In my rearview I watched Nils make eyes at Nora. *He's better looking than her, smarter than her, he's just better*, I thought. They were mismatched. Like fast food and fancy silverware. Or spray cheese and sprouted bread.

"Oh, hey! This is me. I'm up here, on the left," she said, "the green one with the tree." There was a porta potty parked on her front lawn next to a tall stack of aluminum siding. "We're expanding the kitchen. And adding a half-bath."

I turned up her steep driveway and stopped ten feet short of the garage. She kissed Nils on the mouth. *Smooch, smooch.*

"Thanks again, Holly." And then, to Nils, "Call me."

"Will do."

She was gone.

I kicked the car into reverse and started backing up. "Okay, get up here. I am not your chauffeur." Nils scooched from back to front, contorting to get through the tiny space between seats. We were side by side now. Neither one of us talking. I drove quickly back down Nora's twisty street and out onto the main road, where we passed my favorite rock. White and long and crater-faced; like a slice of the moon.

"Okay. What the hell, Nils, *Nora Bittenbender*?"

"So cute."

"Of course. *Cute*. What beats cute?" I snipped.

"Boobs."

"Right . . . of course. *Boobs* beats cute." I glared at him sideways. He had his head turned and tilted back, his hand hanging languidly out the window.

"You don't even know the girl, Holly."

This thing with Nils and girls started junior year with Keri Blumenthal, a pool party, and a stupid green bikini. Then before I could blink, my friend was gone and in his place was this dumb dude who *loved* Keri Blumenthal and lame bikinis and even though I'm *loath* to admit it, this is when things really changed for us. Keri Blumenthal wedged a wall between us. Fourteen days they lasted and still, when they went bust, that dumb wall stayed intact. "She talks like a baby," I said.

"Holly."

"And why does she wear those clothes?"

"Comfort . . . social conventions . . ."

"Not *any* clothes, pervert. Those *particular* clothes."

"Holly. Come on."

"Seriously, what's the deal with her and Epstein? Is that for reals, or no?"

"I dunno . . ."

"I just don't understand why you like her. You're better than—"

"Holly." He sat up really quick and grabbed my hand. "Stop it. Okay?" He tightened his grip and creepy tingles rolled up my arm. "I'm not gonna marry the girl."

I looked back at the road, mimicking Nora's babyish lilt. "You're not?"

Nils dropped my hand. "You're a weirdo, Holly."

I pursed my lips. "At least I'm not a baby with . . . big boobies."

"Weirdo."

I slapped him hard on the arm and turned up my driveway. We both laughed.

I parted ways with Nils and beelined for the fridge. Harry was at my heels begging for food, so I unwrapped a single slice of American-flavored soy cheese, rolled half into a little ball, and dropped the other half on the floor. He inhaled the thing in two seconds flat, not even stopping to chew.

I walked to my bedroom, simultaneously nibbling on my little ball of fake cheese and taking off my clothes, item by item. I slipped on my running shorts and a tank, grabbed Harry's leash, and poked my head into Jeff and Mom's room on my way to the back door. She'd been gone six months and somehow, the entire place still smelled like her: rose oil and castile soap. I don't know how that happens, someone dies and their scent stays behind. Jeff hadn't changed a thing. All her clothes were still on their racks in the closet, her perfume on the vanity, her face creams and make up in the little bathroom off their bedroom. Most days it was easy to pretend she was still around. Out at the store. On a walk. In the garden. Out with Jeff.

So I took the dog out running. Up the canyon, past Ms. Penn's place with that wicker chair she has tied to a rope so it hangs from her tree like a swing; up Pawnee Lane, past Nora Bittenbender's, past Red Rock Road, and out into town. I bought a ginger ale at the Nature Mart and walked back most of the way, trying to keep twigs and rocks out of Harry's mouth.

Later that night, around seven, Jeff came home.

"Hi, Dollface." He kissed my forehead and took a bottle of seltzer out of the fridge. He held it to his neck, then took a long swig, settling into his favorite wooden chair. "What's for dinner?"

"Tacos, maybe? I was thinking I'd drive down to Pepe's. Another night of pasta, I just might hurl."

Jeff laughed his sad little Jeff laugh and kicked off his

loafers. "'Kay, sounds good to me, whatever you want." Then he handed me a twenty. I put Harry in the car because he loves hanging his head out the window at night while I drive, and we sped down the hill, to the beach, to Pepe's, where I bought eight tacos: four potato, two fried fish, two chicken. I kept the warm white bag in my lap on the drive back, away from Harry, and thought about Mom for a second or two. Specifically, her hair: long and thick and dark, like mine. I sang along to a song on the radio I didn't really know the words to, and when my cell rang, I checked the caller ID but I didn't pick up. I didn't recognize the number.

Jeff and I ate in front of the TV that night, watching some cheesy dating reality show that he loves and I hate, but I humor him because he's my dad and his wife is dead and anything that makes him happy now, I'm into. So we finished dinner, I kissed him good night, and then I went out back to The Shack with my cell to listen to the message from my mystery caller. "Hi, Holly," said the voice on my voice mail, "it's Paul. Bennett. I'm just calling to see what you're up to tonight. Gimme a ring." *Click.* My heart shot up to my throat. We'd never talked on the phone. In fact, we'd never really talked.

I held the phone to my chest and considered calling back, I did, but the whole sex-in-his-car-at-the-beach thing had really struck me as a one-time deal. I called Nils instead.

"Hello?"

"It's me."

"You out back?"

"Yeah. Jeff's asleep in front of the TV and I'm bored."

"Be right there. I'm bringing CDs, though, okay?"

"Whatever you say." I flipped my phone shut.

"Holly-hard-to-get. Hi."

Paul and I were standing shoulder to shoulder outside my Chem class. He was wearing a battered old pair of khaki cut-offs, black aviators, and a brash grin. "You don't return phone calls?"

I stared at him, mystified, as he shuffled backward. I shook my head.

"Too bad." He blinked. "What do you have now, Chem?"

"Mm," I managed.

"You stoked?"

"What for?"

"Class." He cocked his head sideways, scanning my face for signs of humor, no doubt. "I'm kidding."

I looked at him blankly. Why were we standing there, talking still?

"Holly?"

"Hmm?"

"Are you okay?"

"I'm fine, yeah. Tired, I guess."

"Well . . . are you busy later?"

I nodded *yes I'm busy, sorry, can't hang out* and watched,

rapt, as he swung his pretty head from side to side. "I don't get you," he said.

I hugged the door frame as a couple of kids tried squeezing past me. "What's to get?" I asked, because seriously, *what's to get?* I was baffled, *really* perplexed by his sudden and obsessive interest in me. I wore ratty Levi's and dirty Chuck Taylors to school every day. I rarely brushed my hair. I had *one* friend besides my dog, and spent nights with my checked-out dad in front of the TV. What about me could possibly hold Paul's interest?

He flashed me one last look, gliding a hand along the wall, then disappearing into a crowd of kids in flip-flops and jean shorts standing around in a big square pack.

Was this some big joke or was I suddenly irresistible? Did I even *like* Paul? Did Paul truly like me? I peeled myself away from the door frame, turned a quick pivot, and shuffled into class.

Nils had his elbows pressed against the black Formica desktop and was fidgeting with some metal contraption with a long, skinny rod. I dropped my books down next to him. "What's that?"

"It's a Bunsen burner." Nils considered me. "What's wrong with you?" He moved sideways, making room. "You look pinched."

I grabbed a stool, dropped my bag to the floor, and plopped down next to him. "Just, no. Just—" I ran a finger over a crooked little heart that had been etched into the side of the desk. "Why Nora? Like, why go after her? Do you like her even?"

"Yeah, sure thing."

"No but, do you *like her* like her?"

"I like her enough." *Ick.* This sort of thing was classic *New Nils*-speak. Nils *post* Keri Blumenthal. Yes, maybe he'd had some experience this past year, and yeah, maybe I hadn't even gone past kissing with anyone pre-Paul . . . *still*, that didn't give Nils the right to be cagey and smug when I needed real, straightforward answers.

"What does that mean?"

Nils looked at me. He shrugged. "She's a nice way to pass the time."

I flinched. "Oh. Duh, of course." Then I opened my Chem book to the dog-eared page and pretended to read. So that was it. Sex. A way for Paul Bennett to pass the time. *Holly-pass-time. Holly-ho-bag.* I pressed my forehead to the crease in my textbook.

"What're you doing?"

"Resting."

"What do you care about Nora Bittenbender, anyway?"

"I don't."

"You sure you're okay?"

I sat up. "I'm fine." I gestured toward the Bunsen burner. "Come on. What the hell are we doing with this thing, anyway?"

"We're making s'mores," said Nils, pulling a misshapen Hershey's Kiss from his pocket and a crushed packet of saltines off the neighboring desk.

"Gross," I said, smiling for real this time, feeling a smidge better. "Just gross."

People warn Alex to steer clear of the twins,
but she wants to be part of their crazy world . . .
no matter the consequences.

TURN THE PAGE FOR A PEEK AT
LAUREN STRASNICK'S

HER AND ME AND YOU

1.

I met Fred first.

At a party on Orchard Ave. that Charlotte Kincaid took me to.

Him: "Need a beer?"

Me: "I've already got one."

"Well, drink up," he instructed. He was pale and skinny (and who wears Docksiders and corduroy?). "When you're ready I'll get you another."

Charlotte and I stood shoulder to shoulder chomping pretzels and watching the drunk crowd rock. Charlotte nursed her canned Bud Light and I picked at a pebble of salt wedged between my two front teeth.

"You're new," he said.

"Right." *You're new.* No question mark.

I'd been in Meadow Marsh a week. I missed home. And

Evie. And Charlotte Kincaid would never be Evie. She was soft-spoken and smelled like baby powder and dryer sheets. She had none of Evie's charm or spark.

"Let's sit," Fred suggested.

"I'd rather not."

Charlotte shot me a look, then wandered away. Where was she going? Bathroom? Food foraging? "I want to be alone," I told him, downing the rest of my beer and grabbing another out of the six-pack on the floor by his feet.

"You're at a party."

I felt my face flush, then twisted the top off the bottle and shoved the cap in my coat pocket.

"You don't really want to be alone. . . ."

True. I wanted to be with Evie. Or home in Katonah with Mom and Dad watching crappy TV. I took a bitter swig of beer and handed the bottle back. "You want the rest?" It was time to go.

"Your backwash?"

"Nice meeting you," I said. I pulled my hat from my bag.

"Wait—you're leaving?"

"Do me a favor? If you see Charlotte Kincaid, tell her I walked home?"

"You can't walk—it's pitch-black and freezing."

"I'll be fine," I said. "My grandmother's place is like, half a mile away."

"You live with your grandma?"

In fact, no. Grams was dead. But I'd just moved twenty-eight miles with my unhinged mother to my grandmother's place in Connecticut. Because my favorite parent, Dad, had done some very bad things with a paralegal named Caroline.

"Hey—"

I pulled on my hat and headed for the door.

"Wait!"

"What?"

"Your name?"

"Alex."

Alex, he mouthed. "I'm Fred."

"Fred, right." I was walking backward now, toward the foyer. "What's with the Docksiders, Fred?"

He looked down, then back up. "You don't like my shoes?"

I smiled, turned, and reached for the door.

2.

My mother was on her back—drunk, messy, her head hanging off the side of the sofa.

"Shit, Mommy." I dropped my keys, my coat, and hoisted her head back onto the couch cushions. "Hey," I said loudly, shaking her shoulders. I checked her pulse, her breath—still living. I grabbed an afghan off the recliner and covered her up, then rolled her onto her side just to be safe. I left a trashcan nearby.

In the morning, I called Evie.

"Yo."

"Hi." She sounded groggy; dreamy.

"You asleep?"

"Sort of."

"Well can you talk?"

A beat. I heard muffled whispering, laughing. Then: "I'll call you back."

"Eves?"

"What?"

"Is someone there?"

"I'll call you later." *Click.*

I chucked my cell onto the floor and the battery popped out. "Crap." I got out of bed, forced everything back in its place, jimmied the window open, and dialed Dad.

He picked up. "Snow."

"I know." I hammered the window open wider and stuck my head outside.

"How's my girl?"

"Freezing." I was inside now. Creeping back into bed. "How's home?"

"We miss you." We: Dad. Chicken, the dog.

"Mom's a real mess, you know."

"Honey."

"Have you broken things off with slutty Caroline?"

"Al."

"Because I'm ready for things to go back how they were."

"Honey, it's not that easy."

"I don't believe you," I said. Then, "Gotta go." I flipped my phone shut and buried myself under piles of covers. I curled my knees to my chest, inspecting a scab on my big toe.

3.

I met Adina the following Monday.

Meadow Marsh High was triple the size of my old school. Stained glass. Brick. Science wing. Student center.

I ate lunch alone at an empty table near the restrooms. French fries and ranch. My fave. I crammed five skinny fries into my mouth and looked up. Hovering overhead? Docksider Fred. With a girl.

"Can we sit?"

The girl wore a tattered black dress with four teensy rosebuds embroidered at the collar. Over that she had on a men's tweed coat. She was frail and blond and made me feel oversize and mannish.

"Is this your girlfriend?" I asked.

They sat side by side and close. The girl pulled five clementines out of her book bag, frowning. "His sister."

"Adina," said Fred, pulling a wad of green gum from his mouth. "Where's your friend?"

"Who?"

"That girl from the party."

"Oh." I shrugged. "Charlotte Kincaid. Yeah, I dunno."

"Orange?" offered Adina, digging her thumbnail into a clementine rind.

"No. Thanks though."

Fred pulled a to-go bowl of Cheerios from his blazer pocket. "Awesome table."

"Are you kidding?"

"Yes," he said, pulling the paper lid off his cereal bowl. "Seriously—next time, find a spot *away* from the bathrooms." He smiled. His freckled face made me want to bake a batch of brownies. Down a gallon of milk.

"Hey, what's your name?" The girl asked.

I redirected my gaze. "Alex."

"Alex." She chewed. "You're from . . . ?"

"Katonah."

"Oh, right." She nodded like she knew all about it. "So, Katonah, why are you here?"

"Ah—" I wasn't sure what to say. *My dad's a raging slut?* "My parents—Well, my dad—" I stopped, starting again: "My mom's from here," I finished.

"Fascinating," Adina deadpanned, angling away from me. "Eat faster," she said to Fred.

I winced, watching her nibble at an orange slice. Fred eyed me apologetically. "You settling in okay?"

I shrugged.

"If you need someone to show you around . . ."

Adina laughed, then slapped a hand over her mouth.

"What? What's so funny?" said Fred.

"No, it's just—" Who knew a giggle could sound so patronizing? "No, nothing. You're cute." She made her eyes into small slits.

"Well, if you're feeling lost," Fred said, ignoring her, ripping a piece of loose-leaf from his binder and scribbling something down. "My number." He smiled, sliding the paper forward.

"Thanks," I said cautiously, watching Adina. She watched me back. "Hey," I said softly. "Who's older?"

Fred took one last bite of cereal and pushed his bowl forward. "We're twins."

"Oh." They looked only vaguely alike. Both blond. Both thin. I wondered briefly what Evie might think of Adina. She'd love her pointy collarbone but would call her names behind her back. *Skeletor. Bobblehead.*

"Hey, Katonah."

"Yeah?"

"Here." She tossed a clementine rind across the table. It landed lightly in my lap.

"What's this for?" I picked it up, inspecting it.

4.

"Mommy, it's three. Have you been downstairs yet?"

The room was a dull black. I pushed back the curtains and cracked the window halfway.

"How was school?"

"Fine."

"Meet anyone nice?"

I sat down on the edge of the bed. "I don't know yet." I shut one eye against the light and watched Mom pull her hair into a tight knot. She used to be pretty. Now she looked worn and pale.

"Did Charlotte show you around?" My mother knew Charlotte Kincaid. She was the daughter of Deirdre Kincaid, Mommy's oldest friend.

"Sort of."

"Nice girl, right?"

"I just felt like giving you something."

"I'm touched?"

"You should be. Those things are precious. You think oranges grow on trees?"

I shrugged.

I could've stayed in Katonah. I *would've* stayed, had I thought my mother could survive the additional blow of me choosing Dad over her. "Come downstairs? I'll make you a snack."

She smiled. "Have you talked to Dad?"

I nodded. "I'm home with him this weekend."

Her face fell. She loved Dad, but Dad loved Caroline. I pushed back her covers and tried tugging her out of bed.

"No honey, not yet." She wasn't always this way. So screwy. Dad broke her. "Gimme a minute, okay?"

I let go and her hand hit the bed with a bounce.

about the author

Lauren Strasnick grew up in Greenwich, Connecticut, now lives in Los Angeles, and is a graduate of Emerson College and the California Institute of the Arts MFA Writing Program. She is also the author of *Nothing Like You* and *Her and Me and You*. Find out more at laurenstrasnick.com.